EllRay Jakes

2 BOOKS IN 1

BY **Sally Warner**

ILLUSTRATED BY
Jamie Harper

VIKING

VIKING BOOKS
An imprint of Penguin Random House LLC, New York

EllRay Jakes Is Not a Chicken! first published in the United States of America by Viking,
an imprint of Penguin Random House LLC, 2011
EllRay Jakes Is a Rock Star! first published in the United States of America by Viking,
an imprint of Penguin Random House LLC, 2012
This omnibus edition published by Viking, an imprint of Penguin Random House LLC, 2022

Visit us online at penguinrandomhouse.com.

Omnibus edition ISBN 9780593527306

Printed in the United States of America

1st Printing

LSCH

Text set in ITC Century Std

EllRay Jakes is NOT a Chicken!

For my long-time editor, Tracy Gates,

with affection and gratitude—S.W.

For Peter and Charles—J.H.

CONTENTS

× × ×

* 1 *

TWO FOR FLINCHING

"Two for flinching," Jared Matthews says at lunch one **MONDAY** in January. *BOP!* He punches me really hard on my right arm muscle—which is not very big, it's true.

It looks like a ping-pong ball, only brown.

"I didn't flinch," I argue, rubbing my arm to make the sting go away.

My name is EllRay Jakes, and I am eight years old. I am the smallest kid in Ms. Sanchez's third grade class, even counting the girls, and Jared is the biggest.

It's like I am made out of sticks, and Jared is made out of logs.

My dad says I'm going to get bigger someday, but when?

"Here's one to grow on, EllRay," Jared's kiss-up

friend Stanley Washington says, his glasses gleaming like mean lizard eyes.

And—**BOP!**

"EllRay *wishes* he would grow," Jared says—because I'm so short. Great joke, Jared.

And then Jared laughs like a cartoon donkey: "**HAW, HAW, HAW!**"

It's just another relaxing lunch on an ordinary day at Oak Glen Primary School, in Oak Glen, California.

× × ×

There is a third grade boys' war going on at our school, but the three kids in the war—Jared Matthews, Stanley Washington, and me, EllRay Jakes—all act like nothing is wrong.

Our teacher, Ms. Sanchez, doesn't have a clue.

Ms. Sanchez is smart about what goes on *inside* her classroom, but she doesn't know what goes on outside—before school and during nutrition break, lunch, and afternoon recess.

And outside is when school really happens for kids.

"Good one, Stanley," Jared says after Stanley insults me, and Jared high-fives him.

"Bad one, Stanley," I echo, trying to make fun of them.

Stanley Washington is like Jared's shadow. He wears glasses, like I said, and he has straight brown hair that flops over his forehead as if it has given up trying.

Jared is chunky and strong, and he has frowning eyes, and his brown hair sticks up all over the place like a cat just licked it.

His hair does whatever it wants, just like Jared.

A couple of girls hop by, holding hands. Jared and Stanley step back, looking all innocent—because girls *tell.* Especially these girls, Cynthia Harbison and *her* kiss-up friend Heather Patton.

"Icky boys," Cynthia calls out over her shoulder.

Cynthia is the cleanest person I have ever met. She is strangely clean.

For instance, Cynthia's fingernails never have any dirt under them. Also, her clothes never get any food, poster paint, or grass stains on them, no matter what. I don't think she has very much fun,

and what's the point in being that clean if it means you never get to have any fun?

Cynthia has short, straight hair that she holds back with a plastic hoop, and Heather pulls *her* long hair back so tight in a ponytail that her eyes always look scared. But maybe Heather really *is* scared—from hanging around mean, bossy Cynthia all the time!

Cynthia is like Jared, only without the hitting.

"Hey, EllRay, why don't you go sit on the grass with the rest of the girls?" Jared asks me when Cynthia and Heather have hopped away to the other side of the playground.

"Yeah, crybaby," Stanley says. "Go sit with the girls."

"I'm not even crying, *Stanley-ella*," I say, pretending *he* is the girl.

It's the best put-down I can come up with on such short notice.

"That's not even my name, so duh," Stanley says.

"**DUH**," I say back at him.

I want to turn around and walk away. But if I do, Jared will probably grab me from the back, tight, and start grinding his knuckles into my ribs.

This is one of his favorite things to do, because from far away, you can't tell anything bad is going on.

Jared's supreme goal is to make me cry someday—in front of the entire class.

So I have to wait for Jared and Stanley to be the ones to walk away first.

I would rather be playing kickball with Corey Robinson and Kevin McKinley, who are my friends, but it's not exactly like I have a choice right now.

"*Duh*," I say again. I don't know why.

Finally, finally, *finally* the recess bell rings, and Jared gives Stanley a friendly pretend-shove, and Stanley gives Jared a shove too, only not as hard, because Jared is the boss. And they walk away without even looking at me.

Like I'm nothing!

"Come on, EllRay," Emma McGraw says as she skips by with red-haired Annie Pat Masterson. "We have Spanish this afternoon, and Ms. Sanchez is going to talk about food. Taquitos, burritos, and enchiladas and stuff. Yum!"

Emma is the second-littlest kid in our class, but she loves to eat. I think it's her main hobby.

"Hurry up," Annie Pat calls out, and she and Emma skip away.

And so I hurry up. But I don't skip, because boys just *don't*. Not at Oak Glen Primary School, anyway.

And probably not anywhere.

Not when they have arm muscles the size of ping-pong balls.

✲ 2 ✲

I CAN'T EXPLAIN

Okay. I can't explain why Jared and Stanley started their war against me, but who cares why the war started? Details like that don't really matter, not when someone is secretly grinding his fist into your ribs.

I know *when* it began, though. It began two weeks ago, right after Christmas vacation.

Why don't I tell somebody what is happening?

Because it wouldn't do any good, and here's why:

1. If the other boys in our class knew about this three-person war, they would take sides, and then it would just turn into a bigger war. But it wouldn't be over for me.
2. If the girls in our class knew, they would whisper and stare, and I hate that.
3. If my mom knew what was happening, she would probably call Jared's mother and complain. And of

course that would only make things worse for me in the long run.

4. If my dad knew about our war, he would **FREAK OUT.** First, he would call Ms. Sanchez or the principal. Then they would make a big announcement to the whole class about fighting, and then the grown-ups would study the problem to death, be-cause studying things is what my dad likes best in the whole wide world.

But there's nothing to study about why Jared hates me. I think he's just bored, and he is taking it out on me.

Or maybe beating me up was Jared's New Year's resolution.

Our war started for no reason, and it will probably end for no reason.

I just have to live through it, that's all.

But the point is, this is a terrible Monday. And I know it sounds dumb, but I am a kid who usually likes Mondays—because Monday gives you a brand-new start.

Monday is like a spelling test that your teacher has just passed out, and you haven't had time yet to make any mistakes. It's like a blank piece of art paper that you haven't messed up. Monday is like the second after your teacher asks you a mental math question in front of the whole class—but you haven't given the wrong answer. *Yet.*

Any good thing can happen on a Monday!

Not this Monday, though.

3

"BEHAVIOR: NEEDS IMPROVEMENT"

"You don't have to keep saying it, Dad, because I already promised," I tell my father that night after dinner, which was pork chops and mashed potatoes, and some kind of vegetable that I spread around on my plate so it at least looked half-eaten.

I am trying to keep my voice calm, steady, and well-behaved.

Dr. Warren Jakes—also known as Dad—is giving me a "talking-to," which is the same talking-to I've been getting from him ever since my progress report came out last week.

"Behavior: Needs improvement," Ms. Sanchez wrote.

Teachers never think about what happens *after* they send home a report card or a note, because writing that comment in my progress report was like telling my dad that his hair was on fire.

My father is a big, strong guy who wears glasses. He is also very smart. He is a college professor who teaches geology in San Diego.

Geology is rocks, basically.

Teaching about rocks must be the most boring job in the whole world. *Do not tell anyone I said this!* But I wish he were a fireman—or a professional extreme snowboarder.

That would be a whole lot cooler, if you ask me.

But even though his job is usually pretty boring, like I just said, my dad and I sometimes get to go on really fun camping trips to Utah, Arizona, and Nevada, where we collect specimens and eat hot dogs and s'mores.

We've seen rattlesnakes and tarantulas and wild pigs called javelinas!

I love to do alone stuff with my dad.

The only bad thing about my dad is that I think he wants me to be a shorter version of him: smart, serious, and sensible.

I think he might even want me to become a geologist some day.

Don't get your hopes up, Dad!

× × ×

"Pay attention, son," my father tells me, scowling. "I'm bringing up this unpleasant subject for a reason. Ms. Sanchez called to say you were bothering your neighbor in class this afternoon."

"Ms. Sanchez *tattled* on me?" I ask.

I am really, really mad at my teacher when I hear this, because you can get in trouble at school for something, and you can get in trouble at home, but you should never get in trouble both places for the same thing.

I think it's a rule.

It ought to be!

Also, Ms. Sanchez never calls my parents on the days when I'm good. So it's not fair *twice*.

"Ms. Sanchez and your mother and I decided to hold regular telephone conferences, ever since your progress report," my dad tells me. "We want to handle problems as each one arises."

"Well, what about if my neighbor *wanted* to be bothered, did you ever think about that?" I ask, angry enough to talk back to my dad. This is never a good idea, even on a good day.

Which this is not.

"Manners," Dad says, almost growling the word.

But my neighbor in class is Annie Pat Master-

son, I want to explain, and she loves it when I make her laugh in class! She's bored, that's why.

"Make that face again," she whispers, and so I do—just to be polite.

But does anyone except Annie Pat thank me? **NO!**

My dad is telling me something else. "And Ms. Sanchez said that you teased Emma McGraw during Spanish, when she tried to say '*arroz con pollo*,'" he says, continuing his invisible list of *Things That My Son EllRay Has Done Wrong*.

He pronounces it right, of course: "*Ah-rose cone POY-yoh.*"

"The way Emma said it was funny," I object, remembering how mad she looked when she kept saying "*polo*" by accident.

And I kept saying "Marco!" like in the swimming pool game. "*Marco! Polo! Marco! Polo!*"

It made me feel good when everyone laughed, even Emma, and it kind of erased the memory of Jared and Stanley grinding my ribs and giving me "two for flinching" at recess.

That's why I did it.

"But listen, son," my dad says, leaning forward. "You cannot joke around if it's going to disrupt the class. The good of the class always comes first."

He's a teacher, so of course he thinks that.

"I know," I mumble.

"But it will be hard to change the way you behave at school," my father says. "So I'm going to make it interesting for you, son."

I look at him and wonder what he is up to. "Interesting, like how?" I ask.

"Interesting, like Disneyland, next Saturday,"

he tells me, smiling. He loosens his tie—yes, my father almost always wears a tie—as if he's about to get on a ride this very minute.

Disneyland!

We went once with relatives, when I was four, and then we tried to go again two years ago, but my little sister got an earache during the drive to Anaheim, which ruined everything. We had to turn around and drive back home, and my dad has been too busy to go again since.

But added to my father's busyness is the fact that he is not the type of person who likes to have fun. Not *regular people* fun.

"Do you think you can keep your nose clean for an entire week, EllRay?" my dad asks. "With no more bad news during telephone conferences?"

"*Keeping my nose clean*" means not messing up.

"Mmm-hmm," I say, nodding. I am pinching my lips together in case I accidentally say something that needs improvement. I don't want my dad to change his mind—because I really, really, really want to go to Disneyland.

I am already choosing what ride I want to go on first. Alfie can go on the baby rides, but I want to go on the scary ones.

I *sort of* want to, anyway.

"Mmm-hmm," I say again, humming my agreement.

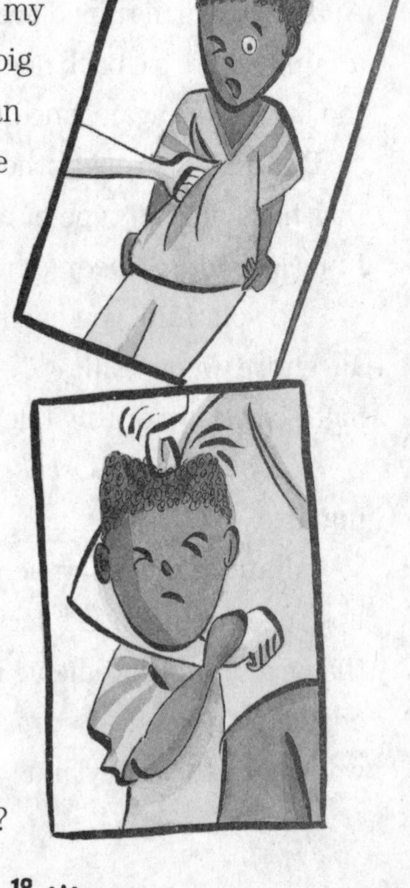

Dad laughs. "Well, okay, then," he says, rubbing my head with the flat of his big hand. "We'll see if you can behave well at school the rest of this week. And that will be the new EllRay Jakes from now on."

The new EllRay Jakes. I guess he's tired of the old one.

But I have a feeling Jared and Stanley will probably hate me even more if I act perfect for a whole week. *Then* what will happen?

BOP, BOP, BOP! Or **GRIND, GRIND, GRIND**.

And then I'll lose my temper, and Ms. Sanchez will find out, and she'll tattle to my parents, and bye-bye Disneyland.

I cannot let that happen.

* 4 *

WHO'S THE BOSS?

"Play dolls with me, *EllWay*," my little sister says a few minutes later, popping her head out of her room as I walk down the hall. She pronounces some words a little bit wrong, but that's okay, because she's only four years old.

"No way, Alfie," I say. "But me and my video game will keep you company." And I go get *Die, Creature, Die*, which my mom thinks is too violent, but it's not.

Last summer, when I was still trying to be nice about playing dolls, mostly to keep Alfie out of my room, a doll head came off in my hand for no reason, and she freaked, like I'd done it on purpose. And I was just trying to be nice.

So, no more playing dolls.

Alfie is very cute. Everyone says so, especially her, but she probably only says that because she

hears it so much. She is golden brown like an acorn, and she wears her hair in three little puffy braids with matching hair-things on the ends. One braid is on top of her head, and there is one on each side.

I can't really describe girls' hair right.

The only trouble with Alfie is the same thing that is the trouble with me: our names. See, "EllRay" is short for "L-period-Ray," which is short for "Lancelot Raymond." And "Alfie" is short for "Alfleta," which means "beautiful elf" in some language from the olden days. Saxon, I think Mom said.

My mom wants to be a fantasy writer some day, that's why we got such goofy names.

My dad should have told her no. Not about wanting to be a writer, of course, but about the names. It's too late now, though.

We have to live with these names *forever*.

"I'm back," I tell Alfie, who is sitting on her rug. She has just finished piling up a stack of doll clothes.

"Which is cuter?" she asks, holding up two little dresses.

"I dunno," I say, trying to settle into my game. "The red one, I guess."

"Okay," she says, and she starts putting the yellow dress on her bare-naked doll.

"How come you even asked me which one is cuter?" I say, feeling a little mad at her, even though I don't really care about the dresses, of course. “So you could do the exact opposite?”

“Nuh-uh,” Alfie says, shaking her head as she tries to cram her doll’s skinny arm through a sleeve. “I just like to hear you talk, that’s all.”

“Oh,” I say, feeling a little better.

“Because nobody talks to me at day care anymore,” she says sadly.

“Oh, c’mon, Alfie. That’s not true,” I tell her—because if there’s one thing about my little sister, it’s that she has a lot of friends.

Friends are very important to girls, I have noticed. They even keep score about them: how many they have, what their ranking is. Friends are like a girl’s very own personal sports team.

It’s different for boys, or at least for me. Sure, I want to have at least one or two friends so there will be someone to hang out with and watch my back, especially lately, but I don’t get all bent out of shape about it.

“Suzette told the other girls not to talk to me,” Alfie says, still looking down at her doll.

Suzette is this bossy little girl in my sister’s day care who likes to keep all the other little girls scared about whether or not she likes them. Big deal.

"She told *everyone* that?" I ask, hating Suzette for one hot second.

"Well, she told Maya and Joelle not to," Alfie tells me. "And Suzette's the boss of our day care, so that's that."

"Aren't your teachers the boss of day care?" I ask her. "I think you should tell them what Suzette is doing, Alfie, and then maybe she'd stop."

"But she might think of something worse," Alfie says, picking up two little doll jackets. "Which one is cuter?" she asks me.

The blue one is cuter, but I don't tell Alfie that. "The orange one," I say, and sure enough, she starts putting the blue one one her doll.

I smile and start playing my handheld video game again.

"Who's the boss of the world?" Alfie asks me, holding her doll up to admire it.

I sigh and press Pause. "No one, I guess," I tell her. "I mean, the world is all divided up, and there are different bosses for different places.

The little places, too. Even Oak Glen has a boss, you know."

"Huh," Alfie says, not asking who that boss is—which is a good thing, because I don't know his or her name. I don't get to vote yet, that's why. "Well," she asks after a couple of minutes, "who's the boss of our family, at least? I vote for Mommy."

And I can't help but laugh, this is such a crazy conversation. "Why not Dad?" I ask her.

"Because whenever we go to Target and Mommy wants something, Daddy says, 'You're the boss, Louise.'"

"I think he's just kidding," I tell her.

"So *Daddy's* the boss?" Alfie asks me.

"No," I say. "I mean, they're both the boss of *us*. Not of each other, I don't think."

"But you're not the boss of me, EllWay," Alfie says, scowling.

"That's okay," I tell her. "Because I don't even *wanna* be the boss of you. It'd be too much work."

Alfie thinks about this for a minute. "Well," she finally asks, "who's the boss of the third grade at school? In your class? Not counting your teacher."

"No one," I say, snapping out the words. But a picture of Jared's head has floated into my imagination like a big ugly balloon.

"There's a boy boss and a girl boss, right?" Alfie asks, trying to work it out.

"Nobody's the boss," I repeat. "But I guess Jared Matthews is the meanest boy, and Cynthia Harbison is the meanest girl."

"Then I hate them," Alfie says, as loyal to me as I am to her.

"You don't have to hate them," I tell her. "But you're lucky you don't have to go to school with them, that's for sure."

Alfie plays in silence for a few quiet minutes, just long enough for me to get into my game once more. Then, sure enough, she thinks of something else to say. "But if Jared and Cynthia moved away," she says, "and so did Suzette, there'd probably just be someone else being the meanest. Or the bossiest."

I look up just long enough to mess up my score.

"I guess you're right," I say, surprised that she could figure something like this out all by herself.

"'Course I'm right, EllWay," she tells me. "Because there can't just be three holes in the world where those mean kids used to be."

"I guess not," I say, giving up and turning off my game.

Sometimes, when I talk to Alfie, I feel like I'm on a merry-go-round that just keeps spinning, no matter how much I want to get off. "I'm gonna go to bed," I tell my spacey little sister. "I think I'm getting a headache."

"Try sleeping with your feet on the pillow," she calls after me. "Because maybe then your headache will get mixed up and go someplace else!"

Let's hope she doesn't want to be a doctor when she grows up, that's all.

5

GLOM

"You were almost late," Annie Pat whispers as I slide into my seat on Tuesday morning. Her red pigtails shine like two orange highway cones.

"I was *almost* late, but I'm *not* late. There's a big difference," I inform Annie Pat, just as Ms. Sanchez begins to take roll.

Annie Pat blinks her dark blue eyes once and looks confused. She can usually count on me to make at least one goofy face or blarty noise first thing in the morning.

Not this week, though.

See, I have a plan, and this morning I timed things just right.

What I did was this: I sneaked into school early, and then I washed my hands for ten minutes in the boys' bathroom so I wouldn't see Jared or Stanley.

It wasn't because I am scared of them, though. I'm just being careful.

My plan is to avoid trouble *all week long* by doing something else or being someplace else whenever Jared or Stanley comes looking for me. But it's just for this week.

Ms. Sanchez starts announcing stuff, as usual, and I start daydreaming, as usual.

But now I have something exciting to daydream about. Disneyland!

And today, **TUESDAY**, the world—or at least Ms. Sanchez's third grade class at Oak Glen Primary School in Oak Glen, California—is going to see me, EllRay Jakes, being a perfect kid.

"Pay attention, Mr. Jakes," Ms. Sanchez says, sounding tired already—and it's not even nine o'clock in the morning.

× × ×

"Hurry up, EllRay, or all the kickballs will be gone," Corey calls out, speeding past me on his way out the door for nutrition break, which is recess with healthy snacks, basically. At least they're *supposed* to be healthy.

"Yeah," Kevin calls over his shoulder. He is moving as fast as a person can humanly move without actually running, because there is *No Running* in the halls at Oak Glen Primary School.

And that is only one of our school's many, many rules.

I sneak out the door while Jared and Stanley

are still getting their snacks out of their grubby backpacks. Jared and Stanley love nutrition break because they love eating, but Corey, Kevin, and I usually eat our snacks—and some of our lunch, too—*before* school, so we'll have more time to play.

And—I'm out the door, and I'm free!

Now, the trick will be to glom onto a group of kids so Jared and Stanley can't yank me aside and grind my ribs, hoist my pants hurting-high, or knuckle my hair.

And I'll have to do the same sneaking away and glomming at lunch, too.

And at recess.

And after school. For three more days.

Glomming is going to take all my attention. I sure hope Ms. Sanchez doesn't expect me to learn anything new this week!

✲ 6 ✲

BUK, BUK, BUK

"Ooo," Jared whispers at lunch. "Here he is, *finally*. What's the matter, EllRay? Scared to be alone with us?"

"Yeah," Stanley chimes in, his voice soft. "**BUK, BUK, BUK!**"

This is his idea of how a chicken talks, I guess, which is just dumb, because chickens do not talk. But basically, Stanley is saying that I'm chicken.

"Shut up," I tell him out of the side of my mouth.

I suddenly realize, though, that I am sitting at the end of the picnic table bench, not somewhere safe in the middle—like between Corey and Kevin, for example. Or even between two girls, if girls sat at our table—which they don't, lately, ever since the food fight.

But that's a whole different story.

Uh-oh. I have made a b-i-i-i-g mistake.

Jared makes a knuckly fist and secretly starts twisting it into my ribs, which are still aching from yesterday's knuckle-grinding. He smiles at everyone else in a fake-friendly way while he is doing it, so they won't know something bad is happening.

Stanley stands back and watches the knuckling, and his eyes are nervous and bright behind his smudged glasses. They look even more lizard-like than usual.

Every single rib I have on that side burns, and

I try not to cringe, but I can feel myself starting to get mad.

Okay. When I lose my temper, three things happen:

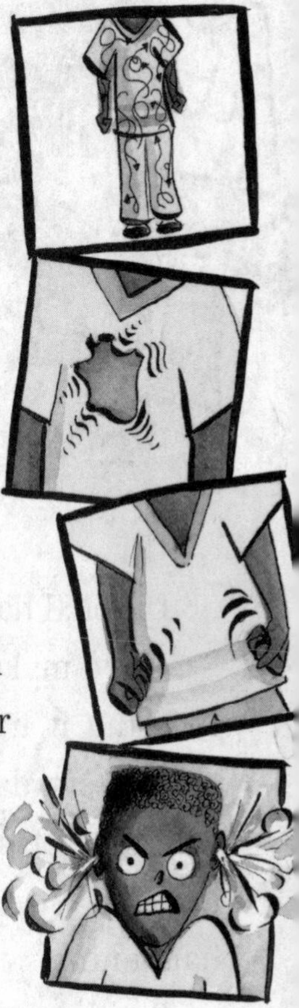

1. First, I can feel all the juices inside my body start racing around really fast.
2. Then my heart starts pounding so hard I can barely hear people talk.
3. And then my hands get clenchy.

Orange sparks may fly out of my ears, for all I know!

Seated across from me, Kevin does not know why I am leaning over so far. "Hey, EllRay, you're going to fall," he says, giving me a friendly smile. Then he goes back to eating his sandwich, a gigantic grinder with pink flaps of meat hanging out. Kevin's hand grips the roll as if it might try to escape from him at any moment.

It would if it could!

"Yeah. Stop crowding, EllRay," Jared tells me,

giving me an extra-hard knuckle twist.

"*Yowtch!* Quit it, Jared," I yell.

"'*Quit it, Jared,*'" Stanley says in a whiny voice, trying to copy me—even though I didn't really whine. Like I said, I yelled. In a manly way.

I try to count to ten, which is what my mom says to do when I start getting mad. *One, two, three, four.* My lips move a little as I silently run through the numbers.

"Oh, look. He's gonna cry. The widdle baby's sad," Jared says, sounding happy. Then he throws back his head and gives his famous **HAW-HAW-HAW** laugh.

"I'm not crying," I say, trying to get to my feet.

I do not want to get into trouble, even at lunch, because the lunch monitor would tell Ms. Sanchez. Then Ms. Sanchez would call my parents, and bye-bye Disneyland on Saturday.

But do I want to go through the rest of my life saying, "***BUK, BUK, BUK***"?

No way!

* 7 *

IT'S DIFFERENT WITH MY MOM

My mom thinks there is always a reason when people—especially kids—are mean, but even though I am only eight years old, I know better.

I think some people—*especially* kids—are mean for no reason.

What about when a mean person shoves someone in the hall? Or "accidentally" knocks the back of that person's head when he is drinking at the water fountain? Or grabs his lunch and plays keep-away with it?

That person does it because he can.

But I don't tell my mom that, because it would only make her sad. Even though she likes to write books about pretend-wonderful things that could have happened in a long-ago time, in real life she is a little bit of a worrywart when it comes to Alfie and me. She wants us never to get hurt.

Just as I think this thought, Mom pops her head around the door to my bedroom. "Can I tuck you in, EllRay?" she asks, smiling.

"Sure," I tell her, scootching over in bed to make room for her to sit next to me. "Good," my mom

says, settling in for a before-bedtime visit, which is secretly one of my favorite things, because:

1. It's not like when I'm at school, where I can never really relax because I don't know what's gonna happen next.
2. And it's not like when I'm with Alfie, where I always have to watch her to make sure she doesn't try to fly down the stairs or something crazy like that.
3. And it's not like when I'm with my dad, where he is either trying to keep me from messing up in the future or scolding me for messing up in the past. Sometimes I think I must be a disappointment to him, he is so important and smart. And strong. And tall.

It's different with my mom. My mom is usually a very relaxing person, and she likes me no matter what. She even likes the *old* EllRay Jakes.

"Your daddy told me about your Disneyland deal," Mom says, arranging my covers more neatly under my chin. "I guess you're pretty happy about that, hmm?"

"Yeah," I say. "If I don't mess it up for everyone.

Don't tell Alfie about it yet, okay? Just in case."

"Okay," Mom promises. "But I know you can do it, honey bun."

"It's—it's kind of like a bribe, though, isn't it?" I ask. "Us getting to go to Disneyland, but only if I'm good. And I thought you guys said that bribing people was wrong. Even bribing *kids*."

My mom laughs a little. "I might have handled things differently," she says quietly. "But whatever works, EllRay—because I want everyone at Oak Glen Primary School to see the same wonderful boy I see whenever I look at you."

"I'm not *always* wonderful," I admit in the dark.

"To me you are," Mom says. "Deep down inside. But—what's going on?"

"Like, in the *world*?" I ask, pretending I don't know what she means.

"Not in *the* world," she says. "Just in *your* world."

"My world's fine," I lie.

But it's the kind of lie that is meant to keep someone from feeling bad, like if a person asks, "*How does my new haircut look*?" and you say,

"*Perfectly normal,*" instead of "*Like somebody went after you with broken kindergarten scissors.*"

"Oh, come on," Mom says in her softest voice. "I know you better than that, EllRay Jakes. And something is troubling you. Is it your progress report?"

"Yeah, it's that," I say, taking the easy way out—because she offered it to me.

Mom leans over to kiss my on my forehead, which is all wrinkled from fibbing. "Well, I wouldn't worry too much," she tells me. "Time passes, doesn't it? I'll bet your work has already improved since Ms. Sanchez wrote that report."

"But it's hard," I say, telling the truth for the first time since she sat down.

"What's hard?" Mom asks.

"Paying attention in class," I tell her. "And remembering all the rules. And sitting in my chair without wiggling. And not bothering my neighbor, even when she wants to be bothered. And not getting mad on the playground. It's hard just being *me*, Mom."

"Oh, EllRay, I know it is," she says, scooping me

into a hug. "But like I said before, being you is also a wonderful thing, honey bun."

"Not so far it isn't," I try to say, but my mouth is smooshed against her sweater and she probably doesn't even hear me.

Mom kisses me on my forehead again and pulls the covers up to my chin. "Well, nighty-night," she says, as if every problem in every world, not just mine, has now been solved. "Close your eyes and go to sleep," she tells me. "Because tomorrow's going to be a beautiful day, EllRay."

× × ×

Today has been a nervous Tuesday for me, I think, lying in the dark, especially because of what happened at lunch. But Mom has made it better, somehow. And I did make it through the afternoon without getting twisted, pounded, or whomped again.

So that's been one whole day without getting into trouble.

Maybe Mom is right. Maybe I can do it!

8

MS. SANCHEZ SAYS

"Quiet, ladies and gentlemen," Ms. Sanchez says on **WEDNESDAY** morning from the front of the class, and she taps her solid-gold pen on her desk.

We all try to look as if we are paying attention, even though half of the class feels like falling asleep because the room is so hot, and the other half—the half with me in it—wants to run outside and play.

It is a beautiful day, just the way Mom said it would be.

"Pay attention, please," Ms. Sanchez says, tapping her pen again. "I have an announcement. We're going to do a science experiment. It's Mudshake Day!"

"But I thought we only had to do science on Tuesdays," Heather Patton says in a really loud whisper, because you're not supposed to talk out loud in class without raising your hand first.

Heather sits behind me in class, and ever since her teenage sister told her she was going to have to cut up a dead frog in science class when she is a teenager, she has hated the entire subject.

Heather doesn't even like frogs that are *alive*, much less dead.

I am not exactly looking forward to cutting up a dead frog, by the way, but it might be interesting—*if* the frog didn't get run over, and *if* it died of old age after leading a long and happy life. For a frog.

"From now on, Heather," Ms. Sanchez says with an ice cube in her voice, "please raise your hand if you have something to say."

"Sorry," Heather mumbles.

"With this experiment," Ms. Sanchez says, sneaking a look at her notes, "we will continue our exploration of soil and its components."

Okay. "Components" means "parts," I happen

to know, only Ms. Sanchez can't just say "parts," for some reason. Probably because it's too simple a word, and we wouldn't get smart if she always said things the simplest way.

So Ms. Sanchez has to say "soil" when she really means "dirt," for example.

Next to me, Annie Pat Masterson aims a smile at Emma McGraw, because they both love science, even when it's just about dirt.

"Here is what your ideal garden soil is made up of," Ms. Sanchez says, and she writes something on the board:

1. 40% SAND
2. 40% SILT
3. 20% CLAY

"Now, who can tell me what this means?" she asks.

Cynthia raises her hand and starts talking before Ms. Sanchez even calls on her, which is typical of Cynthia. "'Ideal' means 'best,'" she says in a very loud voice, and she smiles, using all her teeth, and looks around like she is waiting for us to cheer.

Ms. Sanchez sighs. "That is correct, Cynthia."

she says. "But I was really talking about what the numbers on the board mean."

"Well, *I* didn't know that," Cynthia says, folding her arms across her chest and frowning, which is never a good sign with her.

Cynthia is a girl who knows how to hold a grudge.

The whole class sits in silence for a minute, hoping someone will raise their—her—hand.

In other words, we are counting on Kry Rodriguez to save us.

Kry's real name is Krysten, and she is pretty, with long black hair, and she moved to Oak Glen just before Thanksgiving, and she is very good at math. She slowly raises her hand like there is a red balloon tied to her wrist.

"Yes, Kry?" Ms. Sanchez says, smiling in relief.

Kry clears her throat. "I think the numbers mean that *almost* half of the soil is sand," she says, "and *almost* half is silt, and half of almost-half is clay. Which adds up to one hundred percent."

"Big deal," Cynthia coughs-says into her hand.

Heather laughs to back her up. "Whatever silt is," she mutters.

"And what is silt?" Ms. Sanchez asks in her coldest voice. "Heather? Perhaps you can enlighten us."

"Enlighten" sounds like Ms. Sanchez wants Heather to make us all turn white, which most of my class already is, basically, except for me, Kevin, and two very quiet girls who go to the same church, not mine.

Or else it sounds like our teacher wants Heather to make us light as feathers so we could float up to the ceiling, which would be cool, but no such luck. That's not what Ms. Sanchez means. What "enlighten us" really means is to shine a light on something, only a pretend light, not a real light. In other words, she wants Heather to explain to us what silt is.

I know this, but I do not raise my hand. I don't want to make Jared and Stanley any madder at me than they already are, which they will be if they think I'm showing off by acting smart in class.

"I don't know," Heather mumbles again.

"Anyone?" Ms. Sanchez asks, but no one raises their hand. Not even Kry.

Ms. Sanchez starts to pull her big blue dictionary from the shelf. *"Look it up!"* she usually says when a strange word comes along.

Like every minute, practically.

But all of a sudden, Fiona McNulty slowly raises her hand. This is something that she hardly ever does, because she is the shyest kid in class.

"Yes, Fiona?" Ms. Sanchez says, trying to hide her surprise.

Fiona closes her eyes before she speaks, as if she is about to get a shot at the doctor's office. "Silt is like this teeny tiny dirt that the water moves around, and when the water goes away, the tiny dirt kind of piles up all over the place," she says, squeaking out the words. "My grandpa lives near the Colorado River," she adds, opening one eye as she explains how she knows such an unusual thing.

"Well, that's basically correct," Ms. Sanchez says, after checking her notes once more. "Very good, Fiona."

Fiona blushes.

"And so here is our experiment, people," Ms. Sanchez says. "We have eight glass jars with lids, filled up almost to the top with water, and we have eight mystery soil samples to work with."

Teachers always use words like "mystery" when

they are trying to make something boring sound interesting.

"But—there are twenty-four kids in our class," Cynthia objects, looking around.

"So how many students will be on each mud-shake team?" Ms. Sanchez asks, peeking at her watch. "Tick-tock, people."

"Tick-tock" means "hurry up," when she says it like this.

We all look at Kry. "Three," she says.

"Correct," Ms. Sanchez tells us. "So listen as I call out the teams."

× × ×

"Emma, Jared, and EllRay," she finally says.

Well, it could have been worse, I remind myself. It could have been Stanley, Jared, and EllRay.

"I want each team to carefully pour its mystery soil sample into its water jar," Ms. Sanchez calls out, still reading from her notes.

We let Emma do the pouring, of course, because she's a girl, and girls are always neat. Neater than boys, anyway.

"Now," Ms. Sanchez says, "I am going to come around and add a spoonful of alum to each jar before you start shaking it."

"*AL-um,*" she pronounces it.

Across the room, Annie Pat raises her hand. "Why?" she asks. "What's alum?"

Like I said before, Annie Pat and Emma love science, and they are always full of questions whenever our class does something the least bit scientific.

But that's okay, because it uses up the time.

Ms. Sanchez sighs, as if she was afraid Annie Pat or Emma would ask this question. "Alum has something to do with aluminum," she says. "And for some reason, it makes the soil samples separate more easily into their varying layers of sand, silt, and clay, which will help our experiment. But I'd appreciate it if you'd look up '*alum*' for us tonight, Annie Pat, and fill us all in first thing tomorrow morning."

"Okay," Annie Pat tells her, looking important as she writes down her own personal assignment.

Ms. Sanchez adds a spoonful of white stuff—alum—to each glass jar. "Now stir," she tells us, and Emma hands me the Popsicle stick as if stirring things up is obviously my kind of job. So I do it, because who cares?

"Lids on," Ms. Sanchez says, "and shake!"

That's going to be *Jared's* job, of course. Jared the mighty, Jared the strong.

In about two seconds, he crams the lid on the jar wrong, turns toward me, and starts shaking the mud-filled jar hard, hard, hard.

He practically aims it at me.

Without holding down the lid.

And—**FLOOIE!** There is mud—components of

soil, I mean—all over my best, almost-new T-shirt that has a San Diego Padres logo on it and everything. San Diego is the largest city near Oak Glen.

It is the very same T-shirt I was supposed to wear to the Sycamore Shopping Center this afternoon with my little sister Alfie and my mom, who was going to buy me a corn dog because I got almost all of my Monday spelling words right, for once.

It is the T-shirt Jared looks at with hungry eyes whenever I wear it.

"Oh, no!" Emma cries, holding her cheeks with both hands like the kid in that old movie.

"Oops," Jared says, with the happiest look in the world on his big dumb face. "Sorry, EllRay."

And it's only Wednesday *morning*.

9

WHACKED ON WEDNESDAY

It is now noon, and even though the top half of me is covered with mud, or—excuse me—*soil*, I have made it almost halfway through the week without getting into trouble.

Disneyland, here I come! *Maybe.*

"Did Jared throw mud at you this morning on purpose?" Kevin McKinley asks me.

"Huh?" I say. We are the only ones sitting at the third grade boys' lunch table so far. When the bell rang, I ran outside fast, so I could finish my lunch early and then go wash my hands for half an hour.

I guess Kevin was just hungry.

Kevin takes a big bite

of his big sandwich, chews slowly, swallows the bite, and then takes a long swig of his chocolate milk without even using a straw.

Milk dribbles down my shirt whenever I try that, but I guess today it wouldn't make much of a difference.

Kevin clears his throat. "Corey said that Emma told him it looked like Jared threw that mud on you on purpose during the experiment," he says, and he gets ready to take another bite of his sandwich.

Wow! I didn't know news traveled so fast around here. Or that boys listened to girls. "Why would Jared do that?" I ask, not really answering Kevin's question.

"'Cause he's mean?" Kevin guesses, his mouth full again.

Corey slides onto the bench. "Who's mean?" he asks, opening his lunch sack and peering eagerly into it—even though he's already eaten half of what was inside. All that's probably left is a sack of carrot sticks and the same box of raisins his mom keeps packing every day, even though Corey never eats them.

Those raisins are practically *antiques*.

But don't worry, we'll share our food with him.

"News flash. Jared's mean," Kevin says, filling him in.

"Duh," Corey says, making a face. "Emma says she thought you were going to sock Jared right in the mouth this morning, EllRay."

"Only he's so short he couldn't *reach* my mouth," Jared said, flinging himself so hard onto the bench on the other side of the table that everything shakes: table, benches, antique raisins, little sacks of carrot sticks, us. "EllRay socking me," he sneers in a loud voice. "Like that's gonna happen. Right, Stanley?"

"Right," Stanley says, sliding in next to him.

"You sound kind of like a robot, Stanley," Kevin says thoughtfully, after taking another slurp of his chocolate milk.

Everyone at the table—even Jared and Stanley—is quiet for a second, because Kevin is nearly as big as Jared, so what does that mean in terms of a possible fight? And Kevin is one of those guys who almost never gets mad, but when he does, watch out.

"You got a problem with me, McKinley?" Jared finally asks, because everyone is waiting for him to say *something.*

"Not yet," Kevin says calmly, and he takes another bite of his sandwich.

I wish I could say something like that. Maybe if I was bigger, a *lot* bigger, like half a person bigger, I could.

This talk between Kevin and Jared was almost worth sticking around to hear, but my plan to avoid getting whacked on Wednesday has now been ruined—because I'm sitting here with Jared Matthews and Stanley Washington instead of being in the bathroom washing my hands, and Kevin McKinley can't be *everywhere*, not for the whole rest of the day.

Or the two school days left in the week.

"Oops," Jared says, and then—*after* he says "*Oops*"—he knocks his open carton of milk in my direction. The milk splashes on my peanut butter sandwich and floods the table. It creeps toward the edge of the table—where it will look like I wet my pants if it dribbles onto my lap.

And so even though I don't want to, I scramble to my feet to get out of its way.

"Look at EllRay run," Jared says, laughing, even though I haven't run anywhere—*yet.*

Everyone waits for me to say something or do something to get even with Jared, but I just clamp my mouth shut and think about Disneyland.

It better be worth it.

"***BUK, BUK, BUK,***" Jared murmurs softly, but loud enough for everyone to hear.

"Dude, you owe him lunch," Kevin says, and **SWOOP!** He grabs the sandwich from Jared's big square paw and hands it over to me.

"Oops," I say, and then I drop Jared's sandwich on the ground, and I stomp on it. "Sorry, Jared," I tell him, not sounding sorry at all.

Jared is halfway to his feet, looking really, really mad, and also hungry, but there is no way he can complain without looking dumb in front of everyone, including a few girls—Emma, Heather, and Annie Pat—who are watching us from a nearby table with worried eyes.

After all, Jared made a "mistake," spilling his milk, and I made a "mistake," dropping the sandwich on the ground and stomping on it, so we're even, right?

But I know that somehow, somewhere, I'm going to have to pay *double* for this.

I just hope it's not until next week, that's all.

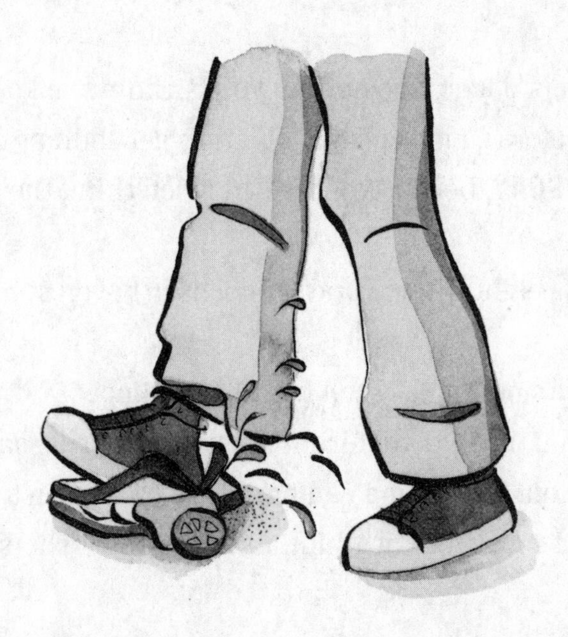

10

THUMPED ON THURSDAY

"Why is Jared so mad at you?" Emma asks me just before I am probably about to get thumped on **THURSDAY**, because of the sandwich thing the day before.

It is eight fifteen, and school hasn't even started yet.

"He's not mad," I tell her. "I don't know."

That is two different answers to the same question, but Emma can handle it. "Why don't you have a meeting with him and find out?" she suggests.

This is a very embarrassing conversation.

Also, boys do not solve their problems by having meetings. That's much more a a girl thing, in my opinion. And all of a sudden, I can feel my juices racing, my heart pounding, and my hands getting clenchy.

In other words, I am about to lose my temper—with Emma!

"Well, why don't you have a meeting with your mom to find out why your *hair* is so curly?" I ask, even though I like curly hair.

Especially Emma's, which is long and brown and tangly and always smells good. I don't know how girls do that.

Emma touches her hair, and her eyes get wide, and she steps back, surprised. "Don't get mad at *me*," she says in a shaky voice. "I was only trying to help, that's all."

"Well, stop trying," I tell her, turning to walk away—because it's time to go wash my hands for a while, and *nobody* can help me.

Especially not a girl.

× × ×

It is now just after lunch, and I am on my way to the front of the class to talk about the three layers of soil in our experiment jars.

But Ms. Sanchez turns her back to the class for a second—and I land flat on my face on the floor.

FWUMP.

It's because I had to walk past Jared, that's why. He tripped me!

Okay. There are three things you can do when you fall flat on your face in front of the whole class:

1. You can pretend you are dead, or at least unconscious. But then your teacher will call the nurse, the principal, and your parents.
2. You can pretend it was a joke, and you meant to fall flat on your face. Only it's hard to do that when you think you might throw up or start crying if you try to talk. And if I start crying in front of the whole class,

Jared's supreme goal will have come true, and I can never let that happen.

3. You can—

"Oh, EllRay, sweetie, are you all right?" Ms. Sanchez asks, racing to my side. I know it's her, because I recognize her shoes.

Ms. Sanchez just called me "sweetie" in front of the whole class.

I will never live this down.

This week just keeps getting more and more terrible!

"'*Sweetie*,'" Kevin whispers, cackling. This will be my nickname from now on, I just know it.

"Uh-h-h," I say, which is supposed to mean, *"Sure, I'm fine!"* Only it's hard to explain that from flat on the floor when there isn't any air in your lungs. I try to sit up.

"Jared *tripped* him," Annie Pat cries.

"On purpose," Emma says.

Oh, great! Emma has already forgiven me for

making fun of her hair, and I didn't even apologize yet. Now I feel worse than before.

Thanks a lot, Emma.

"I did not trip him," Jared objects. "I was stretching, that's all, and EllRay got in the way of my foot. *Ow*," he says a little late, rubbing it.

Ms. Sanchez ignores everyone but me. "Are you all right, EllRay?" she asks again, her voice as soft as a mom's.

"I'm fine," I say, struggling to stand up.

After I am on my feet again, I look around the room. Jared is waiting for me to tell on him, but I don't, and he looks confused.

"Do you think you should go see the nurse?" Ms. Sanchez asks me.

"Nuh-uh," I tell her. "I just want to talk about soil and its components, that's all—so I can get credit for doing this very interesting experiment."

"Well, if you're sure," Ms. Sanchez says, still looking worried.

"I'm positive," I tell her, and I hobble the rest of the way to the front of the class.

* 11 *

BAD VIBES

"I have an announcement to make," a serious-looking Ms. Sanchez says to us later that afternoon, after recess, and we instantly hold still in our seats, because you can never tell. "I've been picking up some bad vibes lately," Ms. Sanchez says, looking hard at us.

We have learned by now that "bad vibes" is her way of saying that something in our class feels wrong to her, but she can't say exactly what.

Hearing this announcement, we all relax a little, because—what else is new? There is always *some* bad vibe floating around our class.

1. Sometimes, one of the girls gets her feelings hurt, or a couple of girls get into their version of a fight, and the whole class suffers. Girls know how to spread their

misery around better than boys, who like to keep things secret.

2. Or sometimes, we hear about something bad that has happened outside of school, in some other kid's family—like someone getting sick, or even someone dying, which is what happened to Corey's grandma before Christmas. That also makes bad vibes, of course, because deep down, we all sort of care about each other. Also, I think we're afraid some of the bad might rub off on us.

3. And when we heard last fall that Ms. Sanchez's dog died, those dead dog vibes made us sad for days. Even kids like me who don't get to have a dog, because Alfie's allergic. Those vibes were the worst of all.

This bad vibe is different, though, because I have a feeling it's about me. But no one except Jared, Stanley, and I knows that—and we're not going to talk.

"Is there anything going on that I should know about?" Ms. Sanchez asks us. "Any problems we should be discussing? Because I wanted our new year to start out right, and it just *isn't.*"

Cynthia's hand shoots up, and Ms. Sanchez calls on her. Cynthia stands up. "Well, *I* didn't do anything wrong," she says loudly. "And neither did Heather."

Heather wiggles in her seat and smiles, happy to be included in anything Cynthia has to say.

But Ms. Sanchez frowns. "I didn't say anyone in this class has misbehaved," she says, trying to clear things up. "I was simply stating that things do not feel right around here."

And she looks at each boy in the class one at a time with her superpower vision.

I guess Ms. Sanchez has narrowed down that bad vibe.

Corey Robinson blushes under his freckles.

Kevin McKinley looks like he wants to run out of the room.

Stanley Washington looks down at his desk and starts polishing his glasses like crazy.

Jared Matthews stares straight ahead, his face as stony as one of the pieces of granite on the display shelf in my dad's home office.

And I, EllRay Jakes, feel as though Ms. Sanchez can tell every single thing that has happened with Jared, Stanley, and me just by looking at my face.

But she can't, I keep telling myself. She *can't*.

Ms. Sanchez shakes her head, looking disappointed in us. "You know you can come to me with any problem, don't you?" she says, speaking to everyone in the class this time.

The girls nod, looking very serious, but all the boys just stare at her. Because—who wants to talk about their problems? Not us!

Boys just want their problems to go away, and the sooner the better.

Now Ms. Sanchez sighs. "Well, my door's always open if anyone has anything they want to share with me," she tells us.

And that's just messed up, because we don't

even know where she lives. So what difference does it make whether her door is open or not?

Also, if she means that her door is always open *at school*, that's not true either. The custodian locks every single classroom door at the end of the day.

And if she means that we can come talk to her during recess, that's not true *either*, because she's always in the faculty lounge. If a kid ever tried to walk in there, the world would probably come to an end.

"Does everyone have that straight?" Ms. Sanchez asks us, and we all nod again.

Especially the boys this time.

Especially Jared, Stanley, and me.

"Good," Ms. Sanchez tells us, not sounding like it's good at all. "I guess you'd better gather your things," she says, "because the buzzer is about to sound. And let's all start out fresh on Friday, shall we?"

And we nod for the third time, except for Cynthia, who says, "We shall! Especially me and Heather!"

You can always count on Cynthia to get the last word.

Only she doesn't, this time.

"It's '*Heather and me*,' Miss Harbison," Ms. Sanchez says, sounding tired, tired, tired.

But I feel pretty excited, because—only one more day to go!

❋ 12 ❋

NOT THAT!

"So, Alfie," my dad says at dinner that night as he helps himself to some rice. "Give us your report."

See, our family has this dinner tradition my mom and dad call "civilized conversation," where each person says the best and worst thing that happened to them that day.

Of course, I have not been telling the truth about my worst things ever since Jared and Stanley started picking on me for no reason a couple of weeks ago.

Alfie twiddles one of her braids, thinking. "Well, my good things are that Suzette wants to be my friend again, and I painted a beautiful picture about a flower," she finally announces.

Suzette is that bossy little girl in my sister's day care, remember?

"You're supposed to choose just one good thing," I tell Alfie, because rules are rules.

And what is the point of a tradition if you do the rules wrong?

"I can choose two things if I want," she tells me, scowling. "Are you saying my beautiful flower picture isn't good?"

"No, he's not saying that, Alfie," my mom says in her *calm-down* voice. "What was your worst thing, honey?"

Alfie scowls, which makes her look like an angry kitten. This is probably not the effect she was hoping for. "My worst thing was when my brother was mean to me at dinner," she tells us.

"All right, then," my dad says. "Moving right along. What about you, Louise?"

It's no fair that my mom and dad have normal names like Louise and Warren when my sister and I get stuck with Alfleta and Lancelot Raymond.

Mom pats her lips with her napkin and looks up at the ceiling. "My good news is that I got a nice rejection letter today for that book I wrote about the enchanted princess who lives in the undersea kingdom," she tells us.

Okay. Now that is just sad, because "rejection" means "no," no matter how good you try to make it sound.

I feel like punching those rejection guys in the nose for insulting my mom!

But instead, I eat another bite of chicken and stare hard at my plate, because one of our rules is that you can't argue about another person's good and bad.

"What did the letter say?" my dad asks.

"That they wanted to see more of my work in the future," Mom tells him, smiling. She looks shy but proud. "And my bad news is that I left the ice cream out on the counter by accident when I got home from the store," she confesses.

There goes dessert, which is bad news for everyone.

"And what about you, son?" Dad asks.

Did I mention that he is still wearing his tie, even though it's just us?

I have been silently rehearsing my answer for the last ten minutes. "My best thing is that I told about the layers of soil in the experiment without messing up," I report. "And the worst—"

"What *about* the layers of soil?" Dad asks, leaning forward as if this is the most interesting thing he has heard all night—which it probably is, because he likes rocks and crystals and minerals better than anything in the world, except us.

"Well," I say, trying hard to remember, "one jar had lots of sand in it, and Ms. Sanchez said that sample was from the desert. And another jar had mostly silt, and that was from some river. And one jar was the perfect mix of sand and silt and clay, which means you could grow stuff in it, Ms. Sanchez said."

"Excellent, EllRay," Dad tells me, beaming. "And what was the worst thing that happened to you today?"

"I dropped my sandwich at lunch," I lie.

Dad looks at me, and his eyes look extra-big behind his glasses. "And that's it?" he asks. "That is absolutely the worst thing that happened to you today?"

I can feel my ears getting hot. "Yes sir," I lie again.

"Then I need to speak to you after dinner, son," Dad says, his voice changing from curious to serious in one second flat. "In my office."

My mom clears her throat, and Alfie looks at me with big sad eyes, like she's feeling really, really sorry for me.

UH-OH.

× × ×

My father is sitting behind his shiny desk, only now he looks like Dr. Warren Jakes, not Dad.

I close the door behind me and listen to the sound of my heart pounding in my ears.

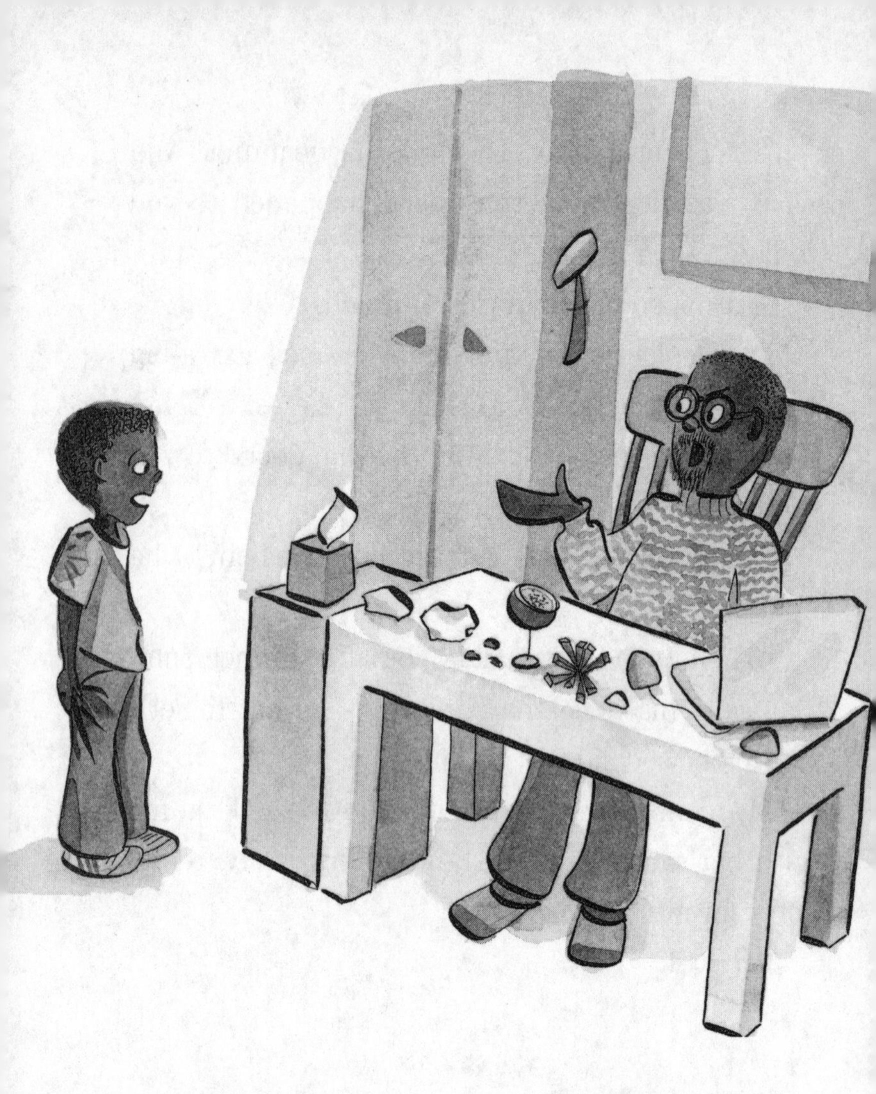

It's no fair to have bad things happen to you at school *and* at home.

It should be one place—at the very most.

I'm not even sure what I have done wrong that my dad is so mad about. It could be so many things!

1. For instance, I didn't brush my teeth this morning, even though I wet my toothbrush so my mom would think I did.
2. And I pulled my bedspread up over the wrinkled sheet and blanket this morning without really making my bed.
3. And I wore a T-shirt that was in the dirty clothes hamper, because I didn't like any of the shirts that were clean.

"Ms. Sanchez called," my dad says. "Just before dinner."

He waits.

This telephone conference thing has gone *too far*.

And why did she pretend she didn't know who was causing that bad vibe?

"But I didn't behave wrong," I say in a croaky, guilty-sounding voice.

I don't even mention Disneyland, because I don't want to give my dad any ideas about canceling our trip. He is the strict kind of dad who might do that.

"I know," my dad says, frowning. "But Ms. Sanchez told me you fell down in class, and she says Jared Matthews might have tripped you on purpose.

She wasn't sure, because her back was turned."

I hold my breath and don't say a word.

"*Did* he trip you, son?" Dad asks gently. "Is there something going on at Oak Glen that we should know about?"

Okay.

When we moved to Oak Glen three years ago, my mom and dad were a little worried, because there aren't that many other families in this town who are African-American. Just about ten or eleven of them, something like that. And at first, my parents were on the lookout for any little thing that would tell them people had some problem with us. But so far, so good—except sometimes I wish there *were* more black kids at our school, just so it would come out even.

Oh, and Alfie told me once that Suzette at day care keeps wanting to touch her braids. But that's a secret, we decided, because we don't want our dad to freak.

He's very sensitive about stuff like that.

"No, nothing," I mumble. "It's okay."

"Speak up, son," my dad reminds me. "Be proud of what you have to say."

"I *am* proud," I tell him, even though my heart is thudding so hard you can almost see my T-shirt jump. "But Jared tripped me by accident, Dad. Accidents happen, right? That's where the expression comes from."

Sure, I could get Jared in trouble right now by telling on him.

Sure, I could even say he's picking on me because I'm black.

But it's not that! Jared would have said something if it was. He is not the type of kid to keep things to himself. That much is obvious.

Anyway, there are plenty of other things that could be make him want to pick on me. Like, I'm the shortest kid in class, so I'm the easiest to pick on.

And I get all the laughs, so maybe he's jealous.

In fact, I'm better at just about everything at school—except being big—than Jared is.

Or, like I said before, there could be no reason at all. Just him being bored because Christmas is over.

"And you're really all right?" my dad asks, looking me up and down—which doesn't take very much time at all, for obvious reasons.

I nod my head.

"But—why didn't you mention it to your mom or me, EllRay?" Dad asks. "I just don't understand. I certainly think falling flat on your face in class is a worse thing than dropping your sandwich at lunch."

"But dropping my sandwich meant I was hungry all afternoon," I explain, still lying my head off. "And you're not supposed to argue about another person's good or bad," I remind him, even though I probably shouldn't.

Dad sighs. "Well, you have a point there," he finally admits. "But I want you to promise that you'll tell your mother or me if this problem with Jared continues, okay? Because we want to nip this sort of thing in the bud."

I'm not exactly sure what that expression means, but I get the general idea. "I promise," I tell him, crossing my fingers behind my back.

I don't like lying to my dad, but in this case, it's for his own good.

Also, it's for the good of Disneyland.

I think I'll go on the pirate ride first.

"Can I leave now?" I ask. "Because I have homework to do, and I don't want to get behind."

My father looks at me for one long minute. Behind his glasses, his brown eyes still look troubled. "All right, son," he says slowly. "If you're sure everything is really okay at school."

"It is," I tell him. But I pause with my hand on the doorknob and look back. "Thanks, Dad," I say, because all of a sudden, for the very first time, it occurs to me that it is probably hard for him to be him, just the way it's hard for me to be me. He's so prickly and proud, and then he's got all those rocks to lug around.

Maybe it's hard for him, anyway.

* 13 *

FWACKED ON FRIDAY

It's **FRIDAY**, and as I walk to school, I realize that I am just about worn out from behaving so well.

I can last one more day, however. And then—***YA-HOO!***

But it takes me only a few minutes at school to realize that all the grown-ups at Oak Glen are now on the alert for trouble between Jared and me. I guess word gets around. Ms. Sanchez's word, anyway—or maybe my dad's. Who knows?

Our principal is greeting kids on the front steps of the school, as usual. He is very tall, and he has a beard, and you can see him from far away—so it is usually easy to avoid him.

But not today.

"Morning, EllRay," he calls out in a booming voice over the heads of the hurrying kids, and I freeze on the second step from the top. He wades through the kids until he reaches my side. "How's every little thing?" he asks me.

Little. Is he making fun of me because I'm so short? I don't think so, but I'm not really sure.

"Every little thing is fine," I say, looking w-a-a-a-y up at him.

I am never growing a beard, that's for sure. He probably has to shampoo it, and then maybe even use a hair dryer on it. And what about when he eats? Do potato chip crumbs get caught in all that hair?

"Well, I'm just checking in," the principal says, scanning me up and down again with his eyes to make sure I'm really okay.

"Okay. Bye," I say.

The principal narrows his eyes, gives me a searching look, and then turns to say, "Morning!" to some other lucky kid.

And I climb the last step and prepare to get fwacked on Friday.

But maybe I won't get fwacked, I think, allowing myself to hope. Maybe grown-ups being on the alert will save me—for this one last day, at least.

And after today, who cares?

× × ×

"You told," Jared whispers, jamming me up against the BEE CAREFUL! WALK, DON'T RUN! poster with bumblebees on it in the hallway.

"Did not," I tell him, even though his chunky arm with orange freckles on it is pressing hard against my chest.

"Did too," Jared mutters, scowling. "The principal said 'Hi' to me this morning in a weird way."

"I didn't tell," I say again. "Ms. Sanchez guessed, I guess. But I didn't say anything to her, or to my parents, either."

"Hello, boys," the office lady says as she walks by holding a mug of steaming hot coffee. She pauses. "Is everything okay?" she asks, looking at me, not Jared.

"Everything's fine," I tell her. "See?" I whisper to Jared when she finally walks away. "I never told *anyone* that you're mad at me for no reason."

"I do too have a reason, and you know it," Jared tells me.

"I do not know it," I say as the kids bounce around us like bumper cars at the county fair. "I never did anything bad to you. In fact, I try to ignore you every chance I get. I'd be doing it now, if I could."

Jared leans in, his green eyes shining. "Well, what about that time you made me look stupid in front of Heather Patton?" he asks, as if this will prove once and for all how right he is to keep going after me.

"*What* time I made you look stupid?" I ask.

What I am really thinking is that he doesn't need any help from me to look stupid in front of *anyone*. But I decide not to say this, because I'm pretty sure it would only make our troubles worse.

"Right before Christmas," he says, getting mad all over again just thinking about it. "You drew that stupid picture of me and then passed it around. And she saw it. And it was right before my birthday, too, and it kinda hurt my feelings."

This last part about the hurt feelings comes out in a mumble.

Okay.

1. First, I barely even remember drawing that picture, it was so long ago.
2. And second, it was a joke.
3. And third, how was I supposed to know it was almost Jared's birthday? It's not like he invited me to his party or anything!
4. And fourth, I am not a very good artist, so it probably didn't even look like Jared.
5. And fifth, what does Jared care what Heather thinks?

And most important of all, *who knew Jared Matthews had feelings*?

Heather Patton is that girl with the too-tight ponytail, in case you forgot. The girl who hangs around with Cynthia, that clean girl I was telling you about.

"I'm sorry if I hurt your feelings," I tell him, actually meaning it—but only a little.

"Shut up about my feelings, dude!" he bellows, forgetting for a second to be quiet, he is so mad.

"What else can I say?" I ask him, shrugging, even though my heart is pounding.

"Nothing," he says, easing off a little as he sees the principal coming toward us down the hall in that fast walk grown-ups do when they don't want to look silly by running.

"Okay, then," I say in a hurry.

"I won't touch you during school today, *tattletale EllRay*," Jared whispers, "but you better meet me in Pennypacker Park right after school, if you know what's good for you. So I can beat you up."

Only Jared could say something like this and think it makes sense, because why would someone know what's good for them *and* want to get beat up?

But you know what? I think I'm going to do it.

I'll go.

And I'm going to **FIGHT BACK!**

Because then, the whole trouble between Jared Matthews and me will be over with once and for all, and we can start living our normal lives again—whatever those lives were like. I can barely remember.

And even if someone catches us fighting, my dad can't yank Disneyland away from me, because *the fight won't be in school.*

It's going to be *after* school

I will have kept my part of the bargain.

✲ 14 ✲

EUSTACE B. PENNYPACKER MEMORIAL PARK

I don't know who Eustace B. Pennypacker is, or was, but he has a terrible park. It's mostly just boring green grass with clover and bees, and a bunch of trees.

You'd think he could have thrown in a playground while he was at it, but ***NO***.

That is why, even though this park is only a block away from our school, kids hardly ever hang out there.

It is probably also why Jared chose the park for our final fight.

No one will see us, and no one will ever find out what happened the afternoon before EllRay Jakes went to Disneyland, sore—but *happy*.

No one except Jared's loyal friend and robot Stanley Washington.

Oops. I forgot about him.

That's okay, though, because even if Stanley takes a swing at me too, I'll be getting whomped so hard by Jared that I probably won't even notice.

And at least I'll be fighting back!

I am sick of looking over my shoulder and washing my hands all the time.

I have gone all day long without telling anyone what is going to happen, because I am *not* a tattletale, no matter what Jared thinks.

Also, it wouldn't do any good, because this fight is between Jared and me—and Stanley, probably, but there's nothing I can do about that.

Jared needs to get even with me because of Heather, crazy as that sounds, and I guess he thinks whaling on me will help.

And if that's what it takes to end our one-sided feud, okay.

× × ×

"Hey, Jakes. Hey, *sweetie*," Stanley yells, popping out from behind a far-off tree like some goofy, floppy-haired jack-in-the-box. He looks either nervous or excited, I can't tell which, and he keeps looking over his shoulder. "Come over here," he says.

I walk over to him as slowly as I can without going backward, because even though I want to get this fight over with, I am not exactly looking forward to it.

Who would be?

"Hey, Stanley," I say, nearing the tree. I am hoping that maybe Jared has decided to call the whole thing off, and Stanley is supposed to tell me.

And then—**SPROING!** Jared jumps down out of the tree like a big old stinkbug landing on an ant, if that's what stinkbugs do.

And we go rolling across the grass.

POW, POW! Jared punches me in the side, right where my poor skinny ribs are sticking out.

And I grab hold of his shirt and try to get in a punch or two of my own.

THUNK! THUNK!

My fist connects first with Jared's nose by accident, and then it sinks into his stomach, and Jared grunts. He is madder than ever now, and a little bit surprised that I am fighting back, judging by what I can see of the look on his face.

I would hit him again, only I never get the chance because we are rolling around on the ground some more, and all our arms are busy.

And all of a sudden, my mouth is full of Eustace B. Pennypacker's memorial grass—and some of his dirt, too, as Jared grinds my face into the lawn. "*Fuh*," I say, trying to spit it out.

"No spitting," Stanley cries, as if he is the referee, and this is supposed to be some really fair fight.

Yeah, right!

I would explain to them that I'm *not* spitting, only I never get the chance.

"I'll teach you not to spit on me," Jared says—

and he wrestles me onto my back and gets ready to spit in my face.

IN MY FACE!

As if spitting on a person will teach that person not to spit!

I would point out how messed-up this is, only I do not get the chance.

There is a roaring sound in my ears, and I shut my eyes and *especially my mouth*, and I get ready for the worst, only the worst never happens.

Instead, the roaring sound grows louder and louder, and I suddenly realize that it is kids, kids, and more kids, and they are swarming around us: Kevin McKinley, and Corey Robinson, who is supposed to be at swim practice, and Fiona McNulty, and Emma McGraw, and Heather Patton, who accidentally started the whole thing and doesn't even know it, and Annie Pat Masterson.

There are other kids here too, from different classes, and I don't even know their names.

How did they find out?

Stanley. I just know it. That's why he was looking over his shoulder!

Maybe he's not so bad after all.

"Get off him, Jared," Kevin shouts, grabbing Jared by the neck of his sweaty red T-shirt. "You're huge compared to EllRay. It's just not right," he yells.

But Jared wriggles away.

"Big meanie," Emma says, aiming a kick or two toward Jared's shins, which I wish she wouldn't do, because how does that make *me* look?

But Emma can't help herself. She is what my dad would call "a hothead." He says it like it's a bad thing.

"Oh, poor Jared," Heather cries out to the excited crowd of kids. "Look, his nose is bleeding!"

And those are the magic words, I guess, especially coming from *her*, because Jared suddenly lets me go.

I scramble to my feet before he changes his mind.

"You bully," Heather says, whirling to face me. "Why don't you pick on someone your own size, EllRay Jakes?"

Which is when everyone starts to laugh.

Including Jared Matthews, luckily!

And *poof,* just like that our fight is over.

* 15 *

SURPRISE

"Everyone all set?" my dad asks us very early the next morning, after buckling Alfie into her car seat, because—we are on our way to Disneyland!

This will be the best treat ever.

And I earned it the hard way. I am so sore I can barely walk—but Disneyland will cure me.

"*I'm* all set," Alfie announces. She is dressed up in her favorite outfit: ruffled shirt, pink skirt, lacy white socks, and pink sneakers. "I'm going to meet Minnie Mouse," she tells us, looking excited, but also a little scared. "And she's famous."

"*Maybe* you'll meet Minnie," my mom tells her, I guess because she doesn't want Alfie to be disappointed if Minnie Mouse is on vacation in Cabo or something.

"I'll meet her, all wight," Alfie says grimly.

And for everyone's sake, I hope Minnie is on the job today.

"Well, let's keep our fingers crossed," Dad says, sounding a lot more excited than I thought he would. He's even wearing a shirt and sweater instead of a tie. "But leave some room, EllRay," he adds. "Because we're picking someone else up."

"Who?" Alfie asks.

"Yeah, who?" I ask.

My dad looks at me over his shoulder and smiles. "It's a surprise," he says, speaking mainly to me.

And it really, really is.

× × ×

"Hey, Jared," I say a few minutes later, trying to make my voice sound normal as Jared Matthews clambers into the backseat of our car. This leaves me sitting in the middle, exactly where I hate to sit.

This is like a nightmare come true.

Jared and I accidentally solve everything all by ourselves, but it's for nothing? We have that stupid fight, but then they throw us together for a whole entire day?

I guess the grown-ups don't know it, but that's like expecting Jared and me to walk across a bridge that we just built out of white paste and Popsicle sticks.

We are **DOOMED!**

"Jared, we called your parents on Thursday night to suggest that you join us," Dad says as Jared buckles himself in. "And they agreed that it was a good way for you and EllRay to get to know each other a little better. Ms. Sanchez thought so, too. But we decided to keep it a secret—from both of you."

Okay. They called Jared's parents on Thursday night—*before* our big fight on Friday in Eustace B. Pennypacker Memorial Park.

Of course, the grown-ups haven't heard about the fight yet, I remind myself. For now, at least, it's still stealth. All they know is that he might have tripped me once. But the side of Jared's nose where I accidentally socked him yesterday afternoon is black and blue, I am secretly glad to see.

"Hey," he says to Alfie and me in greeting, not knowing where to look. He touches his sore nose. "I told my folks I fell off my skateboard," he whispers, before I can even ask.

In the front seat, Mom opens her purse, pulls out her little lipstick mirror, and peeks back at Jared and me—probably to see if we are silently strangling each other yet.

So far so good, Mom. Mostly because I'm still in shock.

"Who's that?" Aflie says, taking her wet thumb out of her mouth and waving it toward Jared with some suspicion.

"Oh, sorry. This is Jared Matthews," I tell her,

making the introduction. "He's in my class at school. This is my little sister Alfleta," I say to Jared, introducing Alfie politely—just in case Mom and Dad are listening, which I'm sure they are. "It means '*beautiful elf*,'" I explain.

"Hi," Jared mumbles to Alfie.

Alfie scowls. "EllWay told me about you one time," she says to Jared. "He said you were the meanest boy in his class."

"*Alfleta*," Mom scolds from the front seat. "That's enough. Behave yourself."

"That's okay, Mrs. Jakes," Jared says. What a kiss-up!

"She didn't mean it, Mom," I fib.

"I did too mean it," Alfie objects loudly. "EllWay and me decided that boy is just as bad as Suzette." I can tell that Jared does not like being compared to a girl, but there's not much he can do about it.

"I thought you and Suzette were friends again," I say to Alfie.

"Oh yeah," she says, remembering. "But maybe not next week."

"Well, that's kind of like Jared and me," I say, hoping to shut her up. "We're okay now."

Temporarily, at least.

"All wight," she says, accepting this.

Jared and I look at each other for a second, but we don't say anything until my dad is on the freeway heading north, and Alfie has gone back to sucking her thumb and twiddling the end of a soft black braid. She stares dreamily out the car window at the hills racing by. She is nearly asleep.

"I know you didn't want me to come," Jared growls, keeping his voice low.

I think hard for a couple of minutes about what to tell him, because if I lie and say that I'm really happy he's here, maybe he will leave me alone for the rest of the year. Or for a few weeks, anyway,

Or I can tell him the truth and take my chances.

"Not really," I finally admit.

"Well, I didn't even *want* to come, when they told me this morning," Jared whispers gruffly. "So don't think you're doing me any favors. I don't owe you, EllRay."

"Everything all right back there?" Dad asks, glancing at us in his rearview mirror.

"Everything's fine," I report. "Alfie's asleep, and we're just talking quietly."

After Dad gets busy driving again, Jared and I exchange glares. "I'm glad Stanley told," he mutters, his voice even quieter than before. "That's why all those kids came running to the park yesterday. They wanted to see you get it, EllRay."

"They did not," I tell him, also keeping my voice low. "They didn't care *what* they saw, as long as it was something exciting, for a change. And anyway, maybe Stanley told because he likes to do stuff behind your back. And all those kids saw was *you*, getting a bloody nose. Even Heather Patton saw it," I remind him. "*You're welcome*," I add, trying for a little sarcasm.

My heart is thunking so hard in my chest that I can practically see it through my San Diego Padres T-shirt, the one Jared wishes he had, but at least I am defending myself again.

I think the days of me washing my hands for no reason are over.

Jared scowls, but he doesn't say anything more.

This is going to be some weird treat, that's for sure. My stomach is doing flip-flops already—and not the good, scary-ride kind.

Great plan, grown-ups! Just when most of the bad feelings between Jared and me were over *because* of our fight, which we both won, in a way, you went and made things worse by trying to make us have fun together.

Thanks a *lot*.

16

TEMPORARY

If there is one thing that no one likes about Disneyland, I remember about twenty minutes after we first walk down Main Street, it is the lines you have to wait in to get on the rides.

Long, boring, zigzagging lines.

Then, when you finally, finally get to the front of the line, all of a sudden there is a crazy scramble to jump on the ride, and then **WHOOSH**, the ride is over.

The *whoosh* part can be really fun, though—even when Jared Matthews is sitting there next to you like a tree stump, which sometimes happens because of the crazy scramble part.

Of course, Mom and Dad were probably planning on Jared going with me on every single ride. They probably imagined that we would slowly learn to like each other, and maybe even become friends, but even parents can't argue when the official ride people shoo you onto a ride when it's finally your turn. Not when there are a thousand people in line behind you.

As the morning goes on, though, even I have to admit that the invisible coating of ice that has been covering both Jared and me—like the candy coating on an M&M—is beginning to melt a little.

But then, just after lunch, "I want Minnie ears,"

Alfie starts whining after we have been in line for twenty minutes for the pirates ride, and Jared and I exchange worried looks.

"She has a meltdown every afternoon," I tell Jared gloomily. "She still takes naps, that's the thing."

"Who are you talking about?" Alfie asks, sounding suspicious.

"You stay in line," Dad tells Jared, Mom, and me. "I'll take Alfie and go find a Minnie hat."

"No, Warren," Mom says. "We'll all go with you. We have to stick together, or someone's going to get lost."

But it's *Disneyland*, I want to tell them as we get ready to lose our very good place in line. How bad could it be if a very-mature-for-his-age kid, like me, got lost? I could live here forever!

"I have an idea, Louise," Dad says. "I think Ell-Ray and Jared can be on their own for a while, if they promise to stick together. We could try it for an hour, maybe, and see how it goes."

We get to be alone? *In Disneyland?* I can hardly believe what I am hearing!

Even Jared is looking excited.

"I don't know," Mom says, looking worried.

"You could lend EllRay your cell phone," Dad suggests gently. "He'll call me on my cell every fifteen minutes to check in."

I'd call every minute if he asked me to!

Jared and I both hold our breath.

"Well, okay," Mom finally agrees as Alfie starts to tug her away from the line. "Here's my phone, EllRay. *Don't lose it.*"

Mom's cell phone is yellow, sparkly, and very girly, which is embarrassing, but I slip it into my deepest pocket and swap excited, happy glances with Jared, my temporary friend.

"We'll meet here in exactly one hour," Dad says, tapping his watch.

"Okay," I tell him.

"Okay," Jared mumbles happily.

And we're off!

× × ×

Being at Disneyland with Jared wasn't so bad, I think sleepily on the way home. In fact, I don't want to exaggerate or anything, but it was really, really fun.

There were no wedgies, no playing keep-away, no knuckle-grinding, no nothing.

And even though something bad will probably happen again next week, especially when the grown-ups hear about the fight at Eustace B. Pennypacker Memorial Park, a fight that to Jared and me is old news, things are okay for now.

And that's good enough for me!

EllRay Jakes

is a Rock Star!

For Ben Haworth —S.W.

For Henry —J.H.

CONTENTS

× × ×

✲ 1 ✲

TALLER

"I grew an inch last weekend," my friend Kevin McKinley announces at lunch on Friday, smiling like it's no big deal. But it is.

Kevin is brown like me, but already he is **TALLER** than I am, so him growing another inch does not seem fair.

Why can't nature make things come out even? I don't get it.

It is Valentine's Day in exactly one week, which means this is almost the middle of February. Just about every kid in Ms. Sanchez's third grade class is outside, including me, because it is the first sunny day we have had in a long time. Even the birds are having fun. Crows are turning circles in the air.

"No, you did not grow an inch in one weekend," Cynthia Harbison says, basically calling Kevin a liar. **"THAT'S IMPOSSIBLE."**

Everyone holds their breath when Cynthia says something like this. She's usually right, and she likes to boss people around. But mostly, she bosses the girls—especially Emma McGraw and Annie Pat Masterson.

Cynthia's dad has a really cool car, though. It's an Audi. And she's very neat, if you like that kind of thing, which I do not.

"It is not impossible to grow that fast," Corey Robinson says, defending Kevin. He is usually pretty quiet, and he has freckles on his face. Corey smells like chlorine all the time.

Corey is a champion swimmer, but he's not that tall. He's a pretty cool guy. In fact, he's *very* cool. He doesn't threaten to beat me up the way Jared Matthews and his best friend and faithful robot Stanley Washington used to do.

Jared is widely known as the meanest kid in our class. He is absent today.

"Yeah," I chime in, because Kevin's also my

friend. "Maybe he hung upside-down all day long both days, and his legs stretched."

As I say the words, I wonder why I didn't think of this first, because I am the shortest kid—including all the girls!—in our class at Oak Glen Primary School in Oak Glen, California, USA.

Hanging upside-down! It's worth a shot, because:

1. I have already tried drinking so much milk that it almost comes out of my nose when I laugh.

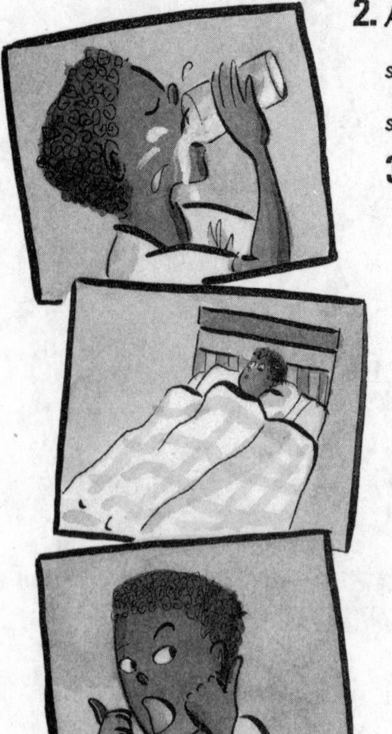

2. And I have tried sleeping straight, not curled up like the shrimp that I am.

3. And I have tried "thinking positive," which is something my dad always recommends. He is a champion positive thinker, unlike my mom, who is a worrywart. She also wants to be a writer of fantasy books for grown-ups, which is why my little sister Alfleta—"Alfie"—and I have such weird names.

My real name is Lancelot Raymond Jakes, in case you didn't know. But please, *please*, just call me EllRay.

My dad's name is Dr. Warren Jakes, and he teaches geology at a college in San Diego. He is very smart, and he is *bigger* than normal-sized, so maybe there is still hope for me.

"I believe you, Kevin," Emma says, daring to argue with Cynthia. "But how do you know you grew an inch?"

"Because my mom marked it on the wall," Kevin tells her—and everyone. "And the last time she did that, I was a whole inch shorter."

"When was that?" Emma asks.

"Last summer," Kevin says. "On the Fourth of July."

Cynthia snickers behind her hand. "Kevin's mom writes on the wall! That's so messy," she says to Fiona McNulty, who is the shyest girl in our class. Fiona has weak ankles, she tells us way too often.

Fiona really admires Cynthia, though. "Yeah. Writing on the wall is so messy," she says, sounding like an echo.

Kevin scowls. "You better not be making fun of my mom," he says in a low and scary voice.

And he's right to say that, because kids can say any bad thing they want about another kid, if they have the nerve, but parents are off-limits.

Also sisters and brothers, unless the kid officially hates them.

Already-tall Stanley Washington frowns and

pushes up his glasses higher on his nose. "But that doesn't make any sense," he says, as if he has been dividing numbers in his head.

"You grew an inch since *last summer*, Kevin," Krysten—"Kry"—Rodriguez says, backing Stanley up. "Not over the weekend."

Kry is very pretty, and she's also good at math and at figuring things out.

"Well, I know *that*," Kevin says. He would be looking mad if anyone else had said what Kry did, but everybody in my class likes Kry.

She's another positive thinker.

"That's what I meant to say the whole time," Kevin continues. "Only somebody interrupted me."

We all turn to look at Cynthia, but Cynthia just shrugs. "Well, who even cares?" she says, straightening the plastic hoop she wears to hold her hair back from her face. "Anyway," she adds like she is making perfect sense, "my dad's taller than Kevin's dad."

That doesn't break the rule about not criticizing parents, but it comes pretty close. We think about it for a while.

"What does that have to do with anything?" Corey finally asks.

"I'm just saying," Cynthia says, satisfied, and Fiona gives her an admiring smile.

"Well, who even cares who's taller?" Stanley says. "Because Jared's dad has a lot cooler stuff than *all* your dads. In fact, he got a brand-new ATV just last week. It's red, and it has flame decals all over it."

"ATV" stands for "All-Terrain Vehicle," and you can ride them *fast* in the desert or at the beach. Lots of places. You don't even need roads.

My dad would probably never buy an ATV, though, because he likes to protect the environment, I guess mostly because the environment has a lot of rocks in it.

I like the environment, too, but I really want to ride in that ATV with the flames.

"Jared's dad might have cooler stuff," Kevin says, defending his father, "but I'll bet my dad has a ton more *money* than him. Because he doesn't spend it all on ATVs, that's why. He saves it."

The girls are looking uncomfortable by now, but none of them walks away.

"Jared's dad has a lot of money, too," Stanley argues. "He wears solid gold jewelry and everything."

And I am thinking two things. First, Stanley is making Mr. Matthews sound like an ATV-driving rap star, if there is such a thing, only he's not. Mr. Matthews is just a regular dad—if you can have someone extreme like Jared for your kid and still be regular.

Second, how did we end up talking about whose dad makes the most money? We were talking about tallness! Then we were talking about *stuff*. How did this lunch period turn into a bragging contest about whose family is the richest—when so many other kids' families are having money troubles?

Maybe even kids here at Oak Glen Primary School.

I already know I could never win this contest, because college professors like my dad don't make a ton of money. Not to hear him tell it. Not compared to some people.

And people who want to write fantasy books for grown-ups make even less.

So how can I compete?

What do *I* have to brag about?

I have to **FIND SOMETHING!**

2

GETTING READY FOR VALENTINE'S DAY

"Psst," Emma whispers later that day. "Are you done with the red marker?"

"Yeah," I say gloomily, snapping the lid on and handing it over. I was drawing a huge ladybug with stingers and fangs, but whatever.

"Isn't this *so much fun*?" she asks.

Valentine's Day is a huge deal at Oak Glen Primary School—for the girls, anyway.

All the boys in school say they hate it, not counting the ones in kindergarten—but I think kindergarten boys only like Valentine's Day because of the treats.

In the third grade, it's different. But at least Valentine's Day is a change, because other than that, nothing interesting happens at school between Christmas vacation and spring break.

At our school, nobody worries about kids' feelings getting hurt because they didn't get enough valentines, which is the way it used to be in the olden days, my mom says. Our school has strict rules about giving people valentines.

1. If you send a valentine to one kid in your class, you have to send valentines to everyone. Even girls-to-girls and boys-to-boys, which is just embarrassing. But you can send funny ones if you want. Funny, but not too gross.
2. Also, the valentines can't have candy or glitter or confetti in them, because of the custodian's temper.
3. And you can't open your cards until the school day is almost over.

But getting ready for Valentine's Day is a pain, because I have to figure out what kind of valentines I am going to send—to the kids in my class, to Ms.

Sanchez, and to my mom and my little sister.

Not to my dad, of course. That's just not us.

Alfie has already informed me that a card to her is *required*, and it had better be good.

We have been making valentines in class today, because Friday is art day. Ms. Sanchez is probably relieved that Valentine's Day is coming, because she can never figure out what to do when we have art. She gloms on to any theme she can: Thanksgiving, President's Day, Arbor Day, you name it. We cover all the Days.

Today is the last Friday we have to work on our cards, though, because like I said, Valentine's Day is in exactly one week.

"I'm making mine all the same, so I'll finish first. I'll win," Stanley tells us. He has a stack of folded construction paper pieces in front of him, and he is scrawling a heart on the outside of each one with a black marker, and a question mark on the inside. He's like a cartoon guy working in a factory, he's going so fast.

By the way, the question mark is supposed to stand for "Guess who?" That's a good way to get around actually signing your name on a valentine.

Just a hint!

"It's not a contest, *Stanley*," Annie Pat Masterson says, drawing the world's fanciest seahorse on one of her cards. Annie Pat is Emma's best friend, and she always fixes her red hair in two pigtails that look like highway warning cones.

"Yeah," Emma says.

"I think everything's a contest," Cynthia argues, not looking up from the card she is working on. "The clothes you wear, how cute your hair is, what you bring for lunch, how late you get to stay up, what your grades are. Only it's different contests for different people. Like, today, my valentines are in the *cute* contest, and I'm winning."

And she draws another unicorn.

Yaw-w-w-n.

Ms. Sanchez is at the end of the table showing Kry how to fold a piece of paper to cut out a perfect heart, so she doesn't hear what Cynthia is saying.

Beside Cynthia, Fiona nods to show how much she agrees with her.

The boys are just listening, because drawing is hard enough, isn't it? You can't talk at the same time.

Well, Stanley can, but look at his valentines.

Kevin is drawing UFOs, and Corey is drawing Christmas trees, because that's what he learned how to do almost perfectly last December.

But he's putting hearts on them.

"That doesn't make any sense," Emma tells Cynthia. "Because how do you know who else is in the same contest as you?"

"You just know, that's all," Cynthia tells her, smiling in a superior way. "At least I do. I know when I'm winning. Like now," she adds, looking at the valentine Emma is working on as if someone just blew their nose on it.

"Yours is good, Emma," Annie Pat says, defending her friend's drawing of a frog sitting on a lily pad. Or a green meatball with eyes, sitting on a plate. "It's *cute*. Here," she adds. "Use my pink marker. It smells like cherries."

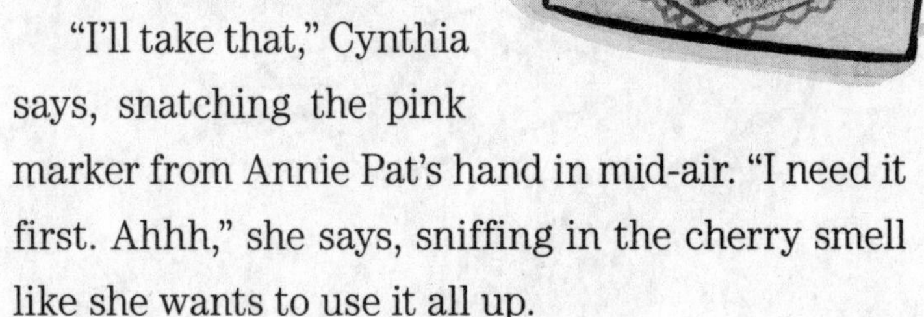

"I'll take that," Cynthia says, snatching the pink marker from Annie Pat's hand in mid-air. "I need it first. Ahhh," she says, sniffing in the cherry smell like she wants to use it all up.

"That's okay," Emma says to Annie Pat, whose dark blue eyes are looking angry. Annie Pat is quiet, but she can be dangerous. "I don't even need pink for a frog," Emma says. "And look," she adds in a whisper, jerking her head toward Cynthia, who is snuffling the marker again.

There is a bright pink dot on the end of Cynthia's stuck-up nose, where she sniffed the marker too close.

It looks like a great big measle!

Annie Pat bites back a smile, and so do Corey, Stanley, and I.

And Fiona's afraid to say anything to Cynthia,

because she and Cynthia aren't exactly equal. Cynthia's already won that contest.

"Now, today is even more fun than before," Emma says, bending low over her frog. Or green meatball. Whatever it is.

"Finish up, people," Ms. Sanchez calls out, sounding happy. I guess she's proud of the perfect heart she just cut out.

And so we do. Finish up, I mean.

✲ 3 ✲

STRAYING FROM THE TOPIC

"Where's Dad?" I ask my mom when Alfie and I sit down to dinner that night—at six o'clock, as usual.

"Oh, EllRay," Mom says, carrying a bowl of spaghetti to the table. "Don't you ever listen to me? I told you this morning. He's speaking at a conference in Utah over the weekend, and then going hiking with a buddy. He'll be home late Tuesday."

"He went to Utah?" Alfie says, almost squawking the question. "Without *me*?"

"Why? What would you do in Utah?" I ask my little sister. "We don't know anyone there."

"I'd have fun, that's what," Alfie says, staring hard at the spaghetti bowl. "I always have fun. Do I have to eat salad too, or can I just eat this?" she asks my mom. “I had carrot sticks for lunch,” she reminds her.

Alfie is an optimist, which means she is another positive thinker. She’s only four, exactly half my age, so she hasn’t had that much experience with life yet.

“You have to eat salad too,” Mom tells her.

“Okay,” Alfie says. “But don’t put anything weird on it. *Please*,” she adds quickly, seeing the look on our mother’s face.

Mom frowns. "Just because it's Friday night and your father is away for the weekend," she says, "that doesn't mean important things such as manners can go flying out the window."

"Yeah, *EllWay*," Alfie says, trying to kick me under the table. That's Alfie-speak for EllRay.

"She was talking to *you*," I tell her, moving my legs away.

"I'm talking to both of you," Mom says, putting some bare salad in a little bowl for Alfie, and then tossing the rest of the torn-up lettuce with salad dressing. "There," she says, sitting down. "You may begin."

And the three of us are quiet for a few minutes as we slurp up our noodles.

Well, my mother doesn't slurp, she winds the noodles around her fork. But that's hard. Only grown-ups can do it.

I clear my throat, because I have something important to say—and my dad being gone means that this is the perfect time to say it. "We should get an ATV," I say, looking at my plate. I try to sound like an ATV is something our family obviously needs, only we have forgotten to buy one before now.

"Yeah," Alfie agrees. "And we should put it in my room so I can watch anything I want. In the middle of the night, even."

Mom dabs at her lips with her napkin, which doesn't even have any spaghetti sauce marks on it, even though we have been eating for almost five minutes. She smiles. "I don't really see that happening, sweetie," she says to Alfie. "You watch enough TV as it is."

"Not a *TV*," I say quickly, before Alfie can start arguing. "An ATV. That's an All-Terrain Vehicle."

"Boo," Alfie murmurs, losing interest.

"I know what an ATV is, EllRay," my mom tells me. "And I can't really see your father buying one, can you?"

"Yes, I definitely can," I say. "It would be useful when we're collecting rocks. You can have an ATV and still love the environment, you know."

"But don't you think your father's more likely to spend any extra money we might have paying bills, or put it into your college savings accounts?" she asks me. "Or even into our retirement fund?" she adds, not looking very hopeful.

Alfie looks up. "Only grandmas and grandpas

retire," she informs us. "They're old. And you're not old, Mommy. Not *that* old."

Alfie's kissing up—for no reason. Just to keep in practice, I guess.

"Well, thank you, Miss Alfie," Mom says. "But your daddy and I will be old, someday."

Alfie looks at her, horrified. "No," she says. "I don't want—"

"An *ATV*," I interrupt, because we are straying from the topic, as Ms. Sanchez so often tells us. "For the desert and the mountains and the beach. Lots of people have them."

"Name one," my mom challenges me.

"Jared's dad," I tell her.

"Ahhh."

She says it like that because Jared and I have had some problems in the past.

In the past few weeks, even.

I can tell my mom thinks I'm jealous of Jared and his ATV. Which I am, a little.

"Jared's lucky," Alfie says sadly, speaking to her last few noodles.

"You're telling me," I mutter.

"Well," Mom says, "I'll pass the suggestion along to your father when he gets home, EllRay."

"How about asking him when he calls tonight?" I suggest—because that way, my dad will have a chance to get used to the idea.

Maybe he won't say no right away, at least.

"If I get the chance," Mom promises. "But don't get your hopes up. And finish your delicious salad."

✱ 4 ✱

KIND OF CRAZY

"Hi, Dad?" I say later that night when my mom hands me the phone. Alfie has already gone to bed, or she'd be hogging the whole conversation.

"Hello, son," my father says. His voice does not sound very far away, which makes me feel nervous because of what I am about to suggest.

"How's the conference going?" I say, wanting to be polite before asking for an ATV when it's not even Christmas or my birthday—and when I can't even drive yet.

"It's going fine," Dad tells me. "I'm presenting my paper tomorrow morning."

"Well, I don't want to bother you," I say, still being super polite. "I just thought maybe we should buy an ATV when you get home. With flames."

I think saying "we" was a good idea, and so was saying the whole thing really fast.

"Flames?" my dad says, as if he has just now started paying attention to what I am saying. "What's this about flames?"

"*Pretend* flames," I say quickly, before he calls the fire department long distance. "They're decals, really. On the sides of our new ATV."

"What new ATV?" Dad asks, sounding confused.

"The one you should buy when you get home," I tell him patiently. "For driving in the desert when we're collecting rocks."

"Why?" my dad asks, shuffling some papers. I can hear him do it!

"You're not even paying attention," I complain.

"Yes I am," my dad says. "You want me to buy a new ATV when we already have a perfectly good Jeep. A classic. It's practically vintage, son."

"That just means old," I tell him. "And our Jeep doesn't have any flames on it. It's rusty, too."

"We can spray-paint some flames on," Dad says, laughing. "Just you and I, EllRay."

"*Really*?" I say, because this sounds like a very un-Dad activity.

"Sure," my dad says. "Why not? If we're careful, and wear masks while we're spraying."

Being careful and wearing a mask is not the way *I* would spray-paint flames on a Jeep, if I had a choice, but it's better than nothing. "And not Alfie?" I ask.

"Not a chance, if you can keep it under your hat," Dad says. This means I should keep my mouth shut and not go blabbing anything about spray paint to my little sister. "This is going to be fun, EllRay," my dad says, like I need telling. "We'll go shopping for the paint when I get home, and you can choose the colors. How does that sound?"

"Good," I say, suddenly feeling like I don't even know my own father. We've hardly ever done anything like this before, that's why. Something alone, and kind of crazy, just to make me happy. "Thanks," I mumble into the phone.

"You're welcome, son," Dad says.

"'Night," I tell him.

"Good night, EllRay. And sleep tight," my dad says.

So, that's good, I think, hanging up the phone.

But I still don't have anything big to brag about.

✲ 5 ✲

MY CRYSTAL-CLEAR IDEA

On Monday night before bed, as my mom is giving Alfie her usual three-towel bath, I wander into Dad's home office to look around—because I kind of miss him.

Also, I usually don't get to go in there unless I'm in trouble.

Even though almost anyone would think that being a geology professor is boring, my dad's office is pretty cool. The wall opposite his desk is completely covered with wood shelves that are so narrow an apple would feel fat sitting there. All my dad's favorite small rock specimens are on these shelves, and each one is carefully labeled. The rocks are from all over the world—Asia, South America, North America—and he collected each specimen himself.

My dad has been *everywhere*.

My favorite shelves are the ones nearest the window, because those hold the crystals. Dad put the crystals there so that sunlight will shine on them first thing in the morning. He says it's a nice way to start the day.

Crystals grow on or in rocks, and they are like diamonds, only better—because they're much bigger, and they come in so many different colors: blue, green, red, orange, and yellow. Even the gray and brown crystals are awesome, not to mention the clear ones that are like ice that never melts.

And crystals look like somebody carved them, only they grew that way. Nature was the carver.

But my dad was the guy who collected them, and he has a story for each one.

My dad's rock specimens are his life scrapbook, practically.

I just wish some of the kids in my class could see them. Maybe then they'd stop bragging about their dads' ATVs, and their money, and their solid gold jewelry, and how everything's a contest that they are winning.

The kids in my class would see how **AWESOME** my dad's crystals are.

And I would win.

That's when I get my crystal-clear idea.

I will borrow six of my dad's crystals—only six!—from his office this very minute, and sneak them up to my room. Then I'll put each crystal in its very own white tube sock for protection, so they won't get knocked around inside my backpack when I take them to school tomorrow.

But before that, I'll spread out the other crystals on my dad's shelf so Mom won't see any empty places in case she goes into the office before he gets home late tomorrow night.

Then tomorrow, Tuesday, I will ask Ms. Sanchez if I can show everyone the crystals, and talk—okay, brag—about them, and she will say yes, because

crystals are so scientific and beautiful. Everyone in my class will be totally **AMAZED** and **IMPRESSED**, and it will be the best Tuesday I ever had in my life. I might even get extra credit!

Then I will take all the crystals home tomorrow afternoon and sneak them back onto the shelf so they will be there when he gets home. He will never know that six of his crystals took a field trip to Oak Glen Elementary School—to make both him and me look good.

There is *no way* this plan can go wrong!

* 6 *

RARE AND VALUABLE

I walk to the front of the class on Tuesday afternoon. I am holding my backpack against my chest with very cold hands.

"Aren't we a little old for show-and-tell?" Cynthia asks in her most sarcastic voice.

"We're never too old to learn something new," Ms. Sanchez says. "And EllRay has some truly beautiful things to show us. Mr. Jakes?" she says, pretending to introduce me to the class.

"Hi," I mumble. I feel very embarrassed and shy, even though I know secret stuff about almost all the kids sitting in front of me:

1. How Jared Matthews sometimes sleeps with masking tape on his hair to make it lie flat.
2. How Stanley Washington has already started saving up for contact lenses.

3. How Emma McGraw sometimes wishes she had a baby brother or sister, or at least a pet.
4. How Fiona McNulty doesn't really have weak ankles, even though she says she does.

"Hi," a couple of kids say, curious in advance.

"What do you have to share with us?" Ms. Sanchez asks, trying to give me a hint about what to say next.

But I have it all planned—and rehearsed. I plunk my backpack on Ms. Sanchez's desk and unzip it. "I brought six rare and valuable crystals to show you today," I say, and I pull out the six bulging tube socks. I set the socks in a straight line on the desk.

"Those are just boys' socks," Cynthia announces to the class. "And they aren't rare *or* valuable. They're smelly, that's all."

"Would you care to wait out in the hall while we listen to what EllRay has to say, Miss Harbison?" Ms. Sanchez asks in her iciest voice.

"Sorry," Cynthia mutters, shooting me a dirty look.

"Okay," I tell everyone. "I brought six **RARE** and **VALUABLE** crystals that my dad went all around the world to find for his collection. He's in Utah right now, in fact, doing important stuff. And here's the first crystal," I say, carefully shaking it out of its sock, which I labeled last night with a permanent marker.

"OOH," a couple of girls in the front row say, staring at the crystal.

"This is called a topaz," I say, holding it up. It

looks like see-through gold, even though topazes are often brown. This topaz's sides are so perfectly smooth that they look like someone polished them. "It's from Brazil, in South America," I tell everyone. "And it got this way all by itself."

"No way," Jared cough-says in the back row.

"Way," I say coolly. "And next is another crystal from Brazil. It's called a tourmaline." And I hold up a beautiful crystal that looks like a piece of the sky, it is so clear and blue. "Tourmalines are also found in some places in the USA, but like I said, my dad found this one in Brazil. Which is where the Amazon River is," I add, inspired. "With piranhas and everything. Not to mention all the snakes."

Fiona McNulty shudders, probably thinking about those piranhas and snakes. The kids in my class are quiet now, and they are staring at the last four tube socks with hungry eyes. They never knew crystals were this cool! They never knew *I* was this cool. Or my dad.

"And here is an aquamarine crystal," I say, holding a blue-green crystal up to the light. It looks like solid swimming pool water. "This crystal is from Pakistan, which is right next to India. Pakistan is pretty dangerous now because of the politics. And it was probably dangerous when my dad went there, too, but he didn't even care!"

I sneak a peek at Jared. He looks impressed by my dad's bravery.

A little, anyway.

Ms. Sanchez taps at her watch, which means that I should hurry up.

"And my number four crystal is called a garnet," I say, holding up a dark red crystal formation.

"Ooh," the girls in the front row say again.

"This crystal is from India, where there are Indians," I tell everyone. "But not the same kind of Indians as in our country, where they are called Native Americans."

Ms. Sanchez should be giving me even *more* extra credit for this, I think—because it's history, geography, and science—all at the same time!

"And my number five crystal is called smoky quartz," I say, holding up a clear gray formation that looks like a wizard could turn it into a crystal ball that really works, if he wanted to. "It's from Nevada, which is only one state away from here," I say. "And I've gone rock-collecting there with my dad, and we saw a rattlesnake once. And also a tarantula," I add, even though we really saw the tarantula in Arizona. I don't have any Arizona crystals with me, but I think that big hairy spider should still count for something.

"Did the snake bite you?" Annie Pat Masterson asks, her dark blue eyes wide.

"Almost," I say, like it was nothing—even though in real life, the snake was in the road and I was in the car.

But if I'd gotten out of the car, it could have bitten me.

If it hadn't already been run over.

"Last but not least," I continue, "is the Herkimer diamond, which is fancy quartz, not really a diamond. It's from Herkimer, New York, which is also in the United States." And I hold up something that looks like it might be the biggest diamond in the world. It's almost as large as an orange! Well, a tangerine, anyway.

Stanley Washington's eyes look like they're about to drop out on the floor, he is so impressed.

"Wow," Kevin McKinley says, looking as though he's about to start clapping.

Corey Robinson seems proud just to know me.

"And that's the end of the crystals I brought," I tell everyone, trying to sound modest. "Only these are just six from my dad's collection—which is *huge*."

And when I pick up the crystals and walk back to my chair, my sneakers can't even feel the floor, my whole body is so happy and proud. I feel like a rock star!

"Thank you, EllRay," Ms. Sanchez calls after me. "And I'll be sure to thank Professor Jakes, too, the next time I see him," she adds.

Uh-oh! Ms. Sanchez is very polite. *Too* polite, sometimes.

"No, that's okay," I tell her quickly. "I'll do it for you."

"Now, gather up your things, boys and girls,"

Ms. Sanchez tells everyone after glancing up at the clock. "Because the final buzzer is about to sound. And don't forget to review your spelling words for the test tomorrow—including these two new words: *crystal* and *formation*." And she writes the two words on the board.

I cannot believe something I brought to school will make it onto an official spelling test. *C-r-y-s-t-a-l. F-o-r-m-a-t-i-o-n.*

I just hope I spell those two words right on the test, that's all!

* 7 *

WHAT AM I SAYING?

Some of the kids in my class crowd around me the very second the final Tuesday afternoon buzzer buzzes—even Jared and Stanley.

This is so cool. My wish has come true! I have never been the most important person in the room before, and it feels *great*.

In fact, I wish this feeling could last forever!

"Can I touch one of the crystals?" Annie Pat asks.

"Sure," I say, because touching a crystal can't hurt it. "Which one?"

"The red one," she tells me. "Red is my new favorite color."

"That's the garnet," I remind her, hauling the lumpy formation out of its sock again.

Annie Pat touches the garnet with her fingertip

as if it might have magical powers. "Um, can I *hold* it?" she asks. "Just for a minute?"

And suddenly, I know how to make this good feeling last a few minutes longer. "You can keep it—"

". . . *for five whole minutes*," I was about to say, but Annie Pat is so excited that she interrupts me.

"Forever?" she asks, like I have just given her a princess crown. She is jumping up and down.

"Sure," I tell her.

What am I saying? That crystal belongs to my father!

"Ooh, what about me?" Cynthia asks, pouncing like a cat going after a grasshopper. "Can I have that baby blue one?"

"It's called a tourmaline," I remind her, my heart crashing around in my skinny chest as I try to think of what to do next. But I can't exactly say no, can I? I mean, I just gave the garnet to Annie Pat!

"And Emma can have the aquamarine crystal," I announce, amazed at my own generosity as I hand over a third crystal.

Three down, three to go. I'm doomed.

"Oh, *thank* you, EllRay," Emma whispers, cradling the blue-green crystal with both hands.

"EllRay?" Ms. Sanchez says quietly, appearing at my elbow as if a genie just rubbed a magic lantern.

"May I have a word with you in private, please?"

"Sure," I say, shrugging to show everyone how not-nervous I am when our teacher asks me this question. I walk over to her desk, where she has been tidying up—and eavesdropping, obviously.

"You're giving your father's crystals away," Ms. Sanchez tells me.

As if I didn't know!

"Well, but it's okay," I lie. "Because my dad said I could. He has lots of them. In fact," I add, "he wants you to have the Herkimer diamond. You can use it for a paperweight or something. But only at home."

"I could never accept such a valuable gift, honey," Ms. Sanchez says.

I hope nobody heard her call me "*honey*," that's for sure.

"It's not a real diamond," I remind her. "But it's way bigger than your engagement ring, so you can see it better. And my father wants you to have it," I repeat.

I sound so sincere!

I hurry to my backpack to get the correct sock.

"He's giving Ms. Sanchez the diamond," I hear some of the remaining kids whisper. They're impressed now, all right! I'll never have to brag again.

"Well, if you're sure," Ms. Sanchez says, her voice still sounding a little doubtful.

"I want the brown one," Kevin says quickly, and so I hand it to him, because—I'm already in so much trouble, why stop now?

And Kevin's my friend, at least.

"I want the gray one," Jared announces, eyeing the last lumpy sock.

And so I hand the smoky quartz crystal to him, almost glad to get it over with. "Sorry, but that's all," I say, showing everyone who's left the six empty socks.

"Aww," a few leftover kids murmer.

"That's no fair," Heather Patton says, scowling.

"Life's not fair," Cynthia tells her, holding onto her tourmaline—*my dad's* tourmaline—as if she is afraid someone is about to snatch it away.

If only I could!

And if only I could turn back the clock—for just ten minutes. Because the wonderful feeling I had five minutes ago has gone. All that's left is the feeling that I am about to yak all over the floor.

What am I gonna tell my dad?

"I hate it when people say life's not fair," Heather says, which is unusual, because usually Heather kisses up to Cynthia like crazy. I almost wish I had another crystal just for her, because I hate that saying, too.

"I need to close up for the day, people," Ms. Sanchez says, standing by the door as she gets ready to turn off the lights. "But don't worry. You'll all be seeing each other in the morning."

We grab our stuff and wander out into the almost-empty hall.

"I'll let you hold my crystal when we get outside," Cynthia promises Heather.

And—it's over.

All except for the part where my dad comes home late tonight.

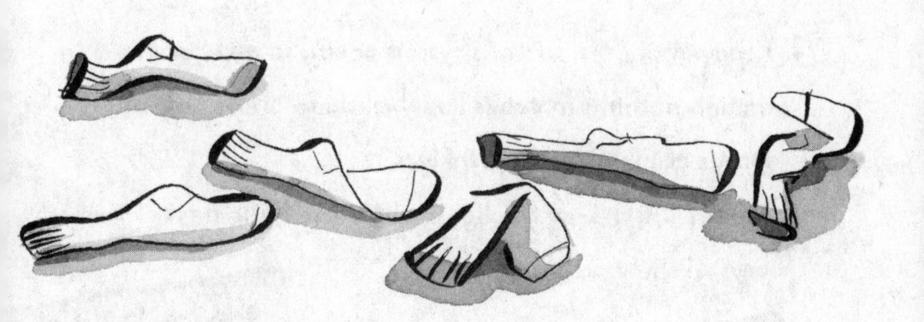

8

DADDY'S HOME!

My dad gets home in five hours, when Alfie and I will already be asleep. I have done everything possible to keep him from noticing that six crystals are missing from his collection.

1. I moved the rest of the crystals again, so now, even though nothing matches its label, there aren't any empty spaces at all left on the shelves.

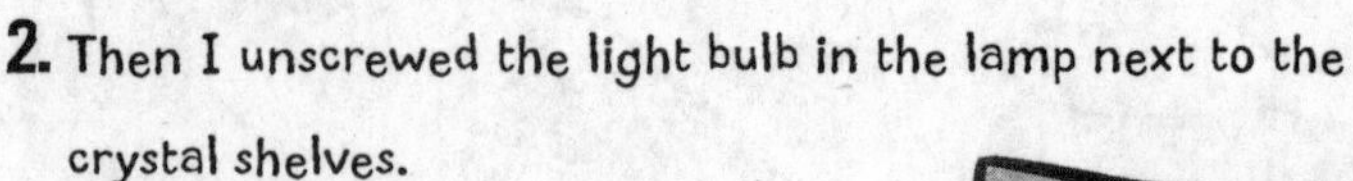

2. Then I unscrewed the light bulb in the lamp next to the crystal shelves.

3. I even got Alfie to draw Dad a big "Welcome Home" sign before dinner and put it in his office. My dad thinks Alfie's this genius artist, and he might be so happy to see the sign that he won't notice anything in the room is missing.

I can barely even remember this afternoon's good feeling, when everybody liked me, but I think the scared and guilty feeling I have now is probably going to last forever.

And that's another example of something that is not coming out even in my life, in addition to the tallness thing.

"Mom says to tell you dinner's ready," Alfie says, peeking into my room, which she says smells like a hamster cage.

Her daycare has a hamster named Sparky, so Alfie's like this big expert now.

Alfie is golden-brown, and my mom always fixes her soft black hair in three puffy braids: one on top, and one on each side of her head. She has about a million little clip-things to hold the braids shut, and the clips go from fancy to extra-fancy. Even though she is four, she still sucks her thumb when she gets worried or tired.

Everyone always says how cute she is, but don't tell *her* that! She's bad enough already.

"Come *on*, EllWay," Alfie says over her shoulder as I follow her down the hall leading to the stairs. "It's macaroni and cheese night."

We always have dinners with no meat in them when my dad is away, because Mom doesn't like cooking, smelling, or even eating meat too much. And that's fine with Alfie, because all she really likes to eat is cheese—and any dessert under the sun.

But me and my dad love meat. We have a lot in common.

I just hope he remembers that if he ever finds out I gave away those crystals.

"Are your hands clean?" my mom asks Alfie and me as we get ready to sit down. Mom's hair looks extra pretty, and she is wearing fancier clothes than the ones she had on when I got home from school. I guess that's because my dad is coming home. They're still smoochy, but only at home, luckily. I mean, that's bad enough.

"They're *basically* clean," I say, hiding my hands behind my back, just in case. I think I washed them after school, but I can't really remember.

"Mine are basically dooty," Alfie says, which means "*dirty*" in Alfie-speak.

"Go wash," Mom tells Alfie and me. "I'll pour you two some icy cold milk to go with your piping hot macaroni and cheese."

Sometimes Mom sounds like a commercial when she talks about food. It's from being a writer, I guess—or from being hungry.

"Guess what? I'm gonna stay up late, until Daddy gets home," Alfie tells me at the downstairs bathroom sink, sudsing up like she's about to perform an operation on someone. "I'm not even a little bit sleepy," she says, passing me the soap.

"Well, I'm going to bed early," I say. I won't go to bed *right* after dinner, or Mom might think I'm sick. But maybe at ten minutes to eight I can start yawning, and then just melt away into my bedroom so I'll be asleep when Dad gets home.

But from down the hall, I hear an unexpected sound.

The front door is opening.

"Daddy's home!" Alfie yells, throwing Mom's fancy hand towel on the floor and racing out of the bathroom.

"Dad's home," I say quietly, looking at my bug-eyed face in the mirror. "And he's almost five hours **EARLY**. Uh-oh."

"We're so happy you caught that earlier flight," Mom says after the hugging has stopped. "And you're just in time for dinner, but I'm afraid it's only mac and cheese."

"Delicious home cooking," Dad says, smiling. "Let me just get rid of this," he tells Mom, gesturing toward his wheelie bag. "I'll put it in my office for now and unpack after dinner."

"No," I shout, surprising everyone. "I mean, *no*," I say again, more quietly this time. "I'll take it upstairs for you, so you can relax."

"Well, that's very thoughtful of you, son," Dad says. "But dinner's ready. You go ahead and sit down. You can help me later."

"But—"

"Go sit down," Dad says, giving me a puzzled look. "I'll only be a minute."

And so I walk into the dining room with concrete feet—and my dad disappears into his office.

* 9 *

MISSING

A few minutes later, Dad comes into the dining room with a weird look on his face, just as Mom has finished passing the mac and cheese to Alfie and me.

"What's wrong?" my mom asks, looking up.

"Were there any strangers in the house when I was away, Louise?" he asks. His voice sounds funny, and I start to feel even more nervous.

"Just the electrician," Mom tells him. "Such a nice young man. He came yesterday to give an estimate on adding that new outlet."

"So he went into my office," Dad says, almost to himself.

"Well, yes," Mom replies. "He had to, to see where the outlet was supposed to go. Why? What's wrong?"

"Some things are missing," Dad says quietly.

My mom almost drops the salad bowl, she is so horrified. "Oh, no," she says.

"We had *robbers*?" Alfie squawks, her brown eyes wide. "Maybe they took some of my toys!" And she races out of the room to check.

"I'll calm her down in a minute. What's missing?" Mom asks my dad. "Not your big computer or the printer, I hope."

"No, they're still there," Dad says. "But some of my crystal specimens are gone. It's not that they're so valuable, mind, but they're valuable to *me*. I collected each and every one of them. Whoever took them tried to cover it up, but I noticed right away."

Naturally. Trust eagle-eyed Dr. Warren Jakes not to miss a thing.

"I just can't believe it," Mom says as the salad bowl droops in her hand. "Why, we've used the Bright Ideas Electric Company ever since we moved to Oak Glen. The young man confided to me that this was his first job, too."

"And it'll be his last, if I have anything to say about it," Dad says, scowling. "We're going to have to go through the entire house after dinner, Louise, to see if anything else is missing—before we call the police and fill out the report."

"Oh, no," my mom says, sinking into her chair. "I can't believe that nice young man did such a thing. Maybe this was a one-time mistake, Warren. Can't we simply call the man's boss and ask that he give the crystals back—and anything else he may have taken?"

"We'll do that as well," Dad says, sounding stern. "But Oak Glen doesn't need people waltzing into other people's houses and helping themselves to whatever they like. I'm calling the company *and* the police," he says again.

I feel like I am frozen in my chair as I imagine that I am the electrician who waltzed—I mean walked—into my dad's office yesterday, just trying to do his job. Here is what he could be thinking pretty soon:

1. I studied really hard at Electrician School, and I made it through all the quizzes and tests, even though I got electric shocks, and not the fun kind. I also had to crawl into spiderwebby tunnels and other scary stuff like that.

2. But I finally graduated and was lucky enough to get a good job, and then I went to some nice lady's house to give her an estimate for putting in a new outlet in her husband's office.
3. I liked the lady so much that I even told her this was my first job!
4. Then I got blamed for stealing—even though I never took a thing. And I got fired.
5. *The End.* Of everything.

I **CANNOT** let that happen.

"Wait!" I say to my mom and dad. "Don't call that man's boss. Don't call the police. There's something I have to tell you."

✻ 10 ✻

ULTIMATUM

"Well, what did you *think* was going to happen when I noticed the crystals were gone?" my dad asks after dinner, when we are alone in his office.

I try not to squirm in my chair, but the tiny bit of macaroni and cheese and salad I was able to eat isn't helping any. It is sitting in my stomach like a softball waiting to be pitched. "I didn't get that far," I finally tell my dad. "I guess I just got carried away with being popular for a change."

"*Popular*," Dad scoffs. He shakes his head in wonder—probably at how dumb the word sounds when I say it.

And that makes me mad, because what kid doesn't want to be popular? Not popular like a TV or rap star, but like a person who other kids admire, at least? So I start talking before I lose my nerve. "You're always saying I should make more friends at Oak Glen," I remind him. "So I just figured—"

"You just figured you'd help yourself to a few of my personal possessions," Dad interrupts, scowling. "That's stealing, EllRay."

STEALING? "No it isn't," I say, my heart thunking so hard in my chest that it's probably bumping into the mac and cheese and salad. "It's not stealing when you borrow something from your own family, Dad," I tell him, hoping this is officially true.

"It's not 'borrowing' when you take something that isn't yours and then give it away," Dad informs me. "And why is it okay to steal from a family member, son?" he asks. "Should you treat someone in your own family worse than you would a stranger?"

"I—I didn't *mean* to give the crystals away," I mumble.

"And I wasn't supposed to find out," Dad says, like he's finishing my sentence for me.

I almost hate my dad right now—because he's making me feel so guilty.

He's probably sorry I'm his son.

"There are lots of aquamarines and topazes in the world," I point out, trying another argument.

"Not ones that I collected when I was in graduate school," Dad snaps. "Not ones I dug out of the earth with my bare hands. I want those crystals back, son."

Now, obviously I am my dad's son. But when he *calls* me "son" like that, it usually means trouble. Not always, but usually.

"I know," I tell him, just for something to say.

"So here's what I'll do," Dad continues. "I'll either call Ms. Sanchez at home tonight and tell her what happened, so that she can make the announcement in class tomorrow morning asking for the prompt return of all six crystals. Or I can come to school with you and make the announcement myself."

"You can't do that," I say, my heart pounding, because—how could I ever live it down? The two friends I have, Kevin and Corey, might never want to talk to me again, I'd look so bad. And so *not honest.*

"I most certainly can," my dad assures me. "But I take it you choose option number one. I'll call Ms. Sanchez this very minute." And he reaches for his cell phone.

Okay. Most parents don't have most teachers' home phone numbers, but it's different at Oak Glen, especially when a kid's behavior "*needs improvement*," which is what Ms. Sanchez wrote on one of my progress reports a few weeks ago.

Ever since then, it's been Communication City around here.

"Don't call her," I say, jumping to my feet. "Let *me* get the crystals back, Dad. It's my mess, and I should be the one to fix it," I add, knowing suddenly that this is the argument that might actually work with him.

Dad leans back in his swivel chair until it creaks, and he slowly puts down his cell phone on the desk. "Do you think you can do that?" he asks.

"Yes," I say, even though in real life, there is no way I can succeed. But at least it will postpone what is sure to be the most embarrassing moment in my life in eight whole years.

"Fine, then," Dad says. "But here's my ultimatum. Do you know what an ultimatum is?" he asks.

"Not exactly," I admit.

"It's when a person says for the final time that you have to do something, or some consequence will happen," my dad explains. "So listen up. You'll ask for the crystals back tomorrow, Wednesday. But if those crystals aren't in my possession by Thursday evening, I'm marching into your classroom first thing Friday morning, and I'm laying down the law."

"But Friday is Valentine's Day, and that's practically a national patriotic holiday," I remind him, hoping this might buy me another day or two.

Because I do not have a plan for getting back those six crystals.

"Do I look like I care?" Dad asks, obviously not expecting an answer. "I feel certain Ms. Sanchez will back me up on this," he says, softening his tone of voice a little.

"I'll get the crystals back," I say, sounding a lot more sure of myself than I am feeling.

"By Thursday afternoon, or I'm coming in on Friday," Dad reminds me.

"All right," I agree in a shaky voice. "Even though Friday is a very important holiday."

"*Valentine's Day*," my dad says, scoffing once more.

He'd better not let Alfie or my romantic mom hear him say it like that!

But I keep this last thought to myself.

* 11 *

EMMA AND ANNIE PAT

It is Wednesday, and it is raining hard again, so Mom is driving me to school. Alfie sits next to me in the back seat, and she won't stop yapping.

"Suzette says we're gonna have a Valentine's Day party in day care," she is telling me. "That's in just two more days. Suzette says we're gonna have pink cupcakes. And I'm making Sparky his very own valentine today."

Suzette Monahan came over for a play date once, and she has to be the bossiest four-year-old kid in the world. She even tried to boss my mom around about the snack they were going to have! Suzette is like Cynthia and Jared *combined*, she's such a pain, but Alfie thinks she's great. When they're not fighting, that is.

And like I said before, Sparky is the day-care hamster.

I think he ought to get a medal, not just a valentine!

"I'm putting a hamster-food heart on the card, so he can eat it," Alfie says.

"That's a good idea," I say, staring out the car window at the wet cars, the wet street, the wet sidewalks, the wet *everything*.

This dark and gloomy day matches my mood perfectly, because—how am I going to get my dad's crystals back? I hate even asking someone to lend me an eraser, much less give me back a present I gave them.

In fact, this is a whole new experience for me.

I am beginning to hate new experiences.

"You're not paying attention to me," Alfie complains. "Mom," she calls out, interrupting my mother's important driving concentration. "Make EllWay pay attention!"

"I can't do that, sweetie," Mom says, signaling

to turn left. "But if you say something really, really interesting, I'm sure he *will* pay attention."

This shuts Alfie up for a few blocks. I guess she's trying to think of something awesome to say, so I take advantage of the unusual calm to remind myself of who has which crystal.

1. Annie Pat has the red garnet.
2. Cynthia has the pale blue tourmaline.
3. Emma has the blue-green aquamarine.

4. Kevin has the golden topaz.
5. Jared has the gray smoky quartz.
6. And Ms. Sanchez has the Herkimer diamond, which isn't really a diamond, even though it looks like one and is bigger than her engagement ring. Way bigger.

How am I going to get them back, ever, much less by tomorrow afternoon?

But I have to, or else my dad will march into my classroom on Friday morning and embarrass me more than I've ever been embarrassed in my life!

"We're here," Mom tells me.

"No, wait," Alfie says, grabbing at my sleeve. "I almost thought of something interesting to say."

"Tell me later, after school," I say, flipping the hood of my yellow rain jacket over my head.

"Good luck today, honey," Mom says, catching my eye in her rear-view mirror.

She knows everything, of course. But she loves me anyway.

That's moms for you.

"Thanks," I tell her, opening the car door. "Because I'm gonna need it."

× × ×

Oak Glen Primary School was built with sunny days in mind, in my opinion, and it's usually sunny in Oak Glen, California. But when it rains, things get a little weird. For example, kids jam together in the hallways before class instead of going out to the playground or the fenced-in yard. And everyone smells wet, and everyone yells.

Then, during nutrition break, we have to eat our snacks in class when it rains—but we can't spill even a crumb, or the mice will come back and Ms. Sanchez will freak again like she did that famous time.

Also, at lunch on a rainy day, everyone has to crowd into the cafeteria instead of eating outside—even the kids who bring their own lunch, like me and most of my friends, because you get to play longer when you bring your lunch.

And during afternoon recess on a rainy day, Ms. Sanchez either plays games with us like "Twenty Questions" or "Simon Says," or, if we "get too squirrelly," as she puts it, she marches us up and down the stairs for exercise with our mouths pretend-zipped shut.

Meanwhile, the real squirrels get to play outside in the rain, and it doesn't do *them* any harm. But nobody thinks of that, do they?

So, basically, rainy days are no fun at Oak Glen, and today, Wednesday, will be the worst one in history. I look around for Kevin or Corey so I will have someone to yell with, at least.

"EllRay," Emma calls out from down the crowded hall, and she and Annie Pat make their way toward me.

"Hi," I say, wondering why Emma wants to talk to me so early. Or at all.

I sneak a look around, but no one is watching, so at least that's okay.

"Thanks again for the aquamarine," she says when she gets to me.

"Yeah," Annie Pat chimes in. "And thanks for the garnet. I showed it to my baby brother Murphy, and he almost tried to eat it, like it was hard red Jell-o. But I didn't let him."

"That's good," I mumble.

"What?"

"*That's good!*" I repeat. "Listen," I say, grabbing

the chance. "I'm really glad you like those crystals and everything, but I gotta get 'em back. It's an emergency," I add, thinking this might make things more convincing.

"What kind of emergency?" Emma asks, her eyes wide. "Are they dangerous?"

"N-n-not exactly," I say slowly, wishing I could say that all the crystals *were* dangerous. Radioactive, maybe, whatever that means. I know it's something bad.

"Well, how come, then?" Annie Pat asks.

She's not mad or anything, she's just asking, and that gives me courage.

"Turns out they were my dad's," I say in a *"Go figure!"* kind of way. Like this was a major surprise to me. "And he decided he needs them back—right away. For important science research reasons," I add, because science is what Emma and Annie Pat like best.

"But I already put mine in my aquarium," Annie Pat says, her red pigtails drooping with disappointment. "So the tetras wouldn't be so bored all day."

Emma frowns, and she plays with a piece of her curly hair. "And I was going to give mine to my mom for Valentine's Day," she tells me.

"She'd probably like a candy bar instead," I say. "A big one. Something chocolate. I'll pay for half of it. And I'll make something else for your fish to look at," I tell Annie Pat, as wet kids push and shove all around us. "Like a LEGO castle, maybe. This is really important, you guys. Can you bring the crystals to school tomorrow?"

"I guess," Annie Pat says sadly, looking as if she would rather not.

"Okay," Emma says. "But we better go, or Ms. Sanchez will yell at us."

Our teacher doesn't yell, but I know what Emma means.

"So let's go," I say, and I cross Emma and Annie Pat off my invisible list of names.

Two down, four to go.

12

TICK-TOCK

Kevin McKinley is the opposite of me in every way except color. Kevin started going to Oak Glen in kindergarten, and I started in first grade. He's tall, and I'm short. He's chunky, and I'm skinny. He has a brother, and I have a sister. He sometimes says "*Present!*" when Ms. Sanchez takes attendance, and Heather Patton usually has to poke me in the back when our teacher calls my name.

I like to daydream, that's the thing.

But we hang together—with Corey Robinson, the kid who swims—so I'm not too nervous about asking Kevin to bring back my dad's topaz. I go up to him during nutrition break. Nutrition break is really just morning recess with food, only today, because of the rain, we're having it in class.

Kevin is over by the window, looking out at the

rain. He keeps dipping his hand into a small crinkly bag of bright orange crackers.

"Hey," I say, unrolling my strawberry fruit leather.

"Hey," he says back, giving me an orange crumb smile.

"I gotta ask you something," I say.

"Okay."

"You know that crystal I gave you? The topaz?" I say.

"Mmm," he nods, chewing.

"I need it back," I say.

"Okay," Kevin says. "I'll see if I can find it in my room."

UH-OH. You should see Kevin's room. I'm surprised he can find his own feet when he gets out of bed in the morning. "I can probably come over this afternoon and help you look for it," I tell him. "I'll call my mom at lunch and ask her."

If kids at Oak Glen have cell phones, which I do not, not yet, they have to leave them in the main office during the day. But there's a pay phone just outside the office, and the lady at the desk will

always lend you the money if you need it. She keeps track, though.

"Okay," Kevin says, smiling, and he reaches into the cracker bag again.

And I cross another name off my invisible list.

Three to go.

× × ×

"Excuse me, Ms. Sanchez?" I ask two seconds after the lunch buzzer has buzzed. "Can I talk to you for a minute?"

Ms. Sanchez tries to hide her sigh. "Of course you *can*, EllRay. You are obviously physically able to speak to me. Are you asking if you *may* speak to me?"

She will never, ever stop correcting us on this one. "*May* I speak to you?"

"You may," she says, sneaking only a tiny peek at her golden watch. "What's up?"

"Well, it's complicated," I say, trying for a thoughtful expression. "But my dad needs that crystal back for his important work. You know, the one I gave you. The Herkimer diamond."

"Ah yes," Ms. Sanchez says with a smile. "That dear Mr. Herkimer."

"Actually, I think Herkimer is a place, not a person," I say, not knowing if she's kidding or not. You can't always tell with teachers, not when they're hungry. "But *anyway*," I repeat, not straying from the topic, "I'm really sorry and everything, but I need that crystal back for my dad's work. Right away, like tomorrow."

Ms. Sanchez narrows her brown eyes and tilts her head, and I can almost feel a question coming. "EllRay," she says slowly, "did you give away those crystals without your father's permission?"

Okay. I could say no, I *did* have his permission, but I know from experience that I'd regret it someday. That lie would come back and bite me.

Also, lying is wrong—but that first reason not to lie is good enough for me.

If I say yes, though, that I *did* give away the crystals without my dad's permission, who knows what will happen?

But if I say nothing at all, I—

"I take it that's a *yes*," Ms. Sanchez says, tapping her foot. "Tick-tock, EllRay."

"*Tick-tock*" means "*hurry up*," when Ms. Sanchez says it.

"Basically," I tell her, looking down at the speckled floor.

"Why did you do it, EllRay?" Ms. Sanchez asks.

Why did I do it? It's funny, I think suddenly—but even my own dad didn't ask me this question. Not exactly. "I don't know," I mumble, still staring at the floor.

"You can do better than that," Ms. Sanchez tells me.

"Well," I say, "I kind of liked it when everyone was paying attention to me in class, for a good reason, I mean, and I wanted them to keep on doing it. And when Annie Pat asked if she could hold the crystal, I just—I got carried away and told her she could keep it."

"Did you *forget* that it belonged to your dad?" Ms. Sanchez asks.

"No," I admit, deciding to keep on telling the truth, because it's the least complicated thing to do, in the long run. "I just wanted the kids to like me a little longer, and giving away those crystals seemed like my only chance."

There is no way she could ever understand about how hard it is for a kid—especially a boy—to be too short to be chosen first for teams, or too bad a speller or mental math guy to win any prizes, or too boring to have an ATV. So I leave those parts out.

"But everyone *already* likes you, EllRay," Ms. Sanchez says, shaking her head in what looks like amazement.

"Not enough."

"Enough for what?" Ms. Sanchez asks. "Did you want to win the popularity contest? Is that it?"

I look up at her. "*Is* there a popularity contest?" I ask, trying not to sound too freaked out. "A real one?"

Don't tell me Cynthia Harbison was right!

"Oh, EllRay," Ms. Sanchez says, shaking her head. "Of course not. But no fear, I'll bring the Herkimer diamond back. You'll have it tomorrow morning. Want me to make an announcement to the class about you needing the other ones returned as well?"

"No, thanks," I say quickly. "I promised my dad that I'd get them back all by myself, by tomorrow. And so far I'm doing okay."

"Tell me if you run into any problems," she says, getting ready to leave. "Is that all?"

"That's all," I tell her. "And thanks, I guess."

"You're welcome, I guess," she says, shooing me out of the room.

So, only two to go.

But they're the worst two: Jared and Cynthia.

13

NO WAY, ELLRAY!

I go up to Cynthia right after lunch. She is in the cafeteria, like everyone else on this rainy day, and she is gathering up her very neat trash while Heather waits for her. "I gotta talk to you," I tell Cynthia.

Cynthia looks up, and she looks suspicious. "About what?" she asks.

"About that crystal I gave you yesterday," I tell her. "The tourmaline. I need it back."

Cynthia laughs. "No way, EllRay!" she says.

She looks pretty serious when she tells me this, and Cynthia Harbison is not exactly known for changing her mind about things.

"Yeah," her loyal friend Heather says, glaring at me. "No way. That rock matches her eyes."

"How come you need it back, anyway?" Cynthia asks.

"Because—because I want to give you something even *better* that matches your eyes," I say, making up a fake reason on the spot.

Now, Cynthia looks like she is doing a mental math problem. "Something even better?" she asks, acting a little greedy, if you ask me.

"Like what **KIND** of thing?" Heather says, sounding as if she wants to make sure her best friend doesn't get cheated.

"You know those beautiful blue flowers they have at the supermarket?" Cynthia asks. "The ones that smell spicy and have glitter on the edges of their zig-zaggy petals?"

Flowers? "Uh, yeah. I guess. I'll give you flowers," I mumble, trying to look around like I'm not looking around.

But I sure hope nobody else is listening in on this nightmare conversation.

"Well-l-l," Cynthia says slowly, "if you bring me

those exact flowers on Friday, Valentine's Day, and you give them to me in front of the whole class, I'll give you back your blue rock."

"It's a crystal," I remind her. "A tourmaline, remember? And I need it tomorrow."

"Whatever," Cynthia says, waving her hand in the air. "I guess I can trust you about bringing me those flowers. But throw away my trash, while you're at it."

"Yeah," Heather says. "Throw away Cynthia's trash."

"Sorry. That's not part of the deal," I tell them, and I walk away fast—before Cynthia *makes* it part of our deal.

Sparkly blue supermarket flowers!

They sound expensive.

I kiss good-bye all the money I've been saving.

* 14 *

SOMETHING REALLY MESSED-UP

It is still Wednesday, and we are having afternoon recess. It has finally stopped raining, so we are outside. I can tell by the expression on Jared's face that word has gotten out that I need the last crystal back—thanks to Emma, Annie Pat, Kevin, or Cynthia, I guess. But I don't blame any of them for blabbing—because what else is there to talk about at Oak Glen Primary School?

Jared is ready for me when I walk up to him on the rain-shiny playground, which smells like wet chain-link fence, and his friend and robot Stanley Washington is standing next to him. A couple of other kids—including Emma and Annie Pat—are hanging around, too, because it's still too drippy to sit down anywhere. "Dude," Jared says to me, after bouncing the red kickball a couple of times

so hard that it **SPLATS** water on Stanley's pants. "Don't even ask, unless you have something good to give me."

Something good to give him. "Like what, exactly?" I ask, trying to think fast.

Flowers are definitely not gonna do it for Jared, not that I'd ever bring him any.

No way!

"I don't know," Jared says. "Something big. Maybe even money, like—five dollars," he says, obviously making up a number on the spot.

Emma and Annie Pat look wide-eyed at each other when they hear this.

"Five dollars," Stanley says, like he's echoing Jared.

“I thought we were friends,” I say, speaking only to Jared—because we *are* friends, at least some of the time. Jared ignored me in both first and second grade, but it’s been like being on a roller coaster in the third grade. A mostly uphill roller coaster, if that means Jared has not been a very good friend to me nearly all that time.

In fact, he tried to beat me up once, but that’s a different story.

“Five dollars,” Jared says again, holding out his hand. “*Now.* Hand it over, EllRay, and I’ll bring your rock back tomorrow.”

“It’s a smoky quartz crystal,” I remind him. “And why would I have five whole dollars with me now, in my pocket?” I ask. “You know we aren’t allowed to bring that much money to school.”

“Okay, then you should make EllRay do something else,” Stanley says to Jared, really excited now. “Something *worth* five dollars. Something really messed-up. Like—EllRay should have to go into the girls’ bathroom. When there’s a girl in it!”

“Classic,” Jared says

“Ooh,” Emma says, and Annie Pat covers her mouth with her hand, she is so shocked—because it is terrible for a boy to go into the girls' bathroom.

It's probably even against the law!

Also, there aren't just third graders at Oak Glen, there are fourth, fifth, and sixth graders, too. And some of those older girls look pretty tough. They're like grown-ups, practically—and they're *big*.

They could squash me like a **BUG**.

But I need that crystal back.

Behind Jared's back, Emma waves her arms to catch my eye, and she makes an "Okay!" circle sign to me with her thumb and pointer finger.

"Okay," I hear myself say to Jared. "I'll do it. Let's go."

15

SCREAMING AND YELLING

"What's the plan?" I whisper to Emma as she and I march across the darkening playground toward the school building.

I don't like having a girl help me, but I'm desperate. I just hope she actually *has* a plan. Emma has been known to get carried away sometimes and promise stuff she can't deliver.

It's because she wants good things to be true, that's the thing.

"Annie Pat ran ahead to empty out the downstairs bathroom," Emma whispers back. "So she'll be the official girl in the girls' bathroom. And I'll stand guard at the door when you go in, so you'll be okay in there. No one will dial 9-1-1 or anything."

"But isn't that cheating?" I ask. "Because Jared wants me—"

"Nuh-uh," Emma interrupts, shaking her head as we scurry along. "It's not cheating. And who cares about what Jared wants? How nice is he being to you?"

Girls care a lot about being nice. Boys care about not getting beat up.

Also, I care about not staying in trouble with my dad.

"There you are," Stanley says in the hall outside the downstairs girls' bathroom. A couple of fifth-grade girls have just hurried out, looking like they are about to gag.

Stanley is almost rubbing his hands together like a cartoon bad guy, he is so happy with his fiendish plan.

"Yeah," Jared says. "Here we are. So let's see you go in there and wash your hands, EllRay! *Slowly*. And then I'll bring that rock back tomorrow."

"It's a crystal," I say again as I stand up straight and get ready to push open the heavy door with the big GIRLS sign on it.

"Whatever, dude," Jared tells me. "Go for it!"

× × ×

Annie Pat is laughing quietly inside the otherwise empty bathroom. I'm scared even to look around the place, since it is so much against the rules for me to be in here. But I do take a peek.

It looks pretty much the same as the boys' bathroom, only messier. I guess when girls are alone, they're neat. When they're together, watch out!

No wonder our custodian has a bad temper.

"What's so funny?" I ask Annie Pat, my heart pounding so hard I can hear it.

"I told those big girls I was about to barf all over the floor, and they *ran*," she tells me, still giggling. "Now, wash your hands, or at least run the water, and I'll start screaming and yelling so Jared will think he's getting a really good deal out of this. *Eeeee!*" she wails in a high and horrified voice just as I get the water running.

It sounds so real that I turn to stare at her, my heart pounding.

"OUT," she roars, in a different, sixth-grade-sounding voice this time. "This is the *girls'* bathroom, you dummy! Let's get him!"

"Yeah, get him," she says again in a different voice.

Annie Pat should be in the movies or something, she's so good.

I wave my wet hands in the air to shut her up, grab a paper towel to dry my hands, slam-dunk the towel into the trash, and hustle out the bathroom door—into the main hall, where it looks like Emma has just told some little first-grade girls that they have to wait another minute before using the bathroom.

"But I *can't* wait!" one of them is squealing as she jumps up and down in distress. So I hold the door open for her like a gentleman.

"Thanks," she and her friend say, racing into the bathroom.

"He did it," Stanley says, almost looking disappointed.

"You did it," Jared says, slapping my hand. "Those girls in the bathroom were really *mad*! It sounded like they were gonna get you good. You got your rock, dude," he adds, heading off down the hall. "Tomorrow."

"It's a *crystal*," I yell after him—even though another rule around here is no yelling in the halls.

But they were right—I did it! And I'll get all six crystals back.

"Congratulations," Emma says, as if she can read my mind.

"Mr. Jakes?" a lady's voice says, and I turn around, my worn-out heart thudding hard once more.

A woman steps out of the doorway opposite the girls' bathroom. I think she's one of the fifth grade teachers, and she's been spying on us. Listening in, anyway.

"Would you care to explain yourself?" she asks. "What on earth were you doing in the girls' bathroom?"

Emma and Annie Pat look like statues, they're so scared. But they don't have to worry. I'm not gonna get them in trouble, too. I owe them.

And even if I didn't owe them, I wouldn't say a word, because—this is my fault.

I started the whole crazy thing when I gave away my dad's crystals.

Just because I wanted something to brag about.

"Cat got your tongue, Mr. Jakes?" the lady asks, staring at me hard, like she really thinks there might be an invisible cat hanging from my mouth.

"I guess," I mumble.

"Hmph," she says, almost snorting. "Well, come

along with me, young man, and we'll see what the principal has to say about this."

The principal!

Not again.

I was only trying to make things right with my dad, and now:

1. I have to make Annie Pat something cool to put in her aquarium so her fish won't be bored.
2. I have to give Emma money for half a candy bar for her mom.
3. I have to wade through all of Kevin's junk after school.
4. And I have to bring Cynthia very expensive-sounding flowers tomorrow, on an official romantic day for girls, and she wants me to give them to her in front of the whole class, which I can't even stand to think about doing.
5. And on top of all that, I'm in trouble with the principal?

I will never look another crystal in the face again for as long as I live!

16

OOPS

"Well, Mr. Jakes—so we meet again," the principal says, smiling.

He's actually smiling! I guess he *likes* having kids dragged into his office.

Okay, I wasn't really dragged, but I might as well have been. It's not as if I have a choice about being here.

"Please take a seat," the principal says.

I'm so scared that I forget his actual name. I can spell principal, though, because Ms. Sanchez always reminds us, "The principal is your pal, do you see? The word ends in P-A-L." Like that's a really fun thing. **HAH**.

The principal does try to be nice and say hi to every kid in the morning. He usually calls us "Mister" and "Miss," probably because he thinks that will make us act better.

But I had to go into his office once already this year, and that was one time too many, in my opinion.

And—*do you honestly think my dad's not gonna hear about this?*

"So, EllRay," the principal says, petting the side of his beard. "I hear you strayed into the girls' restroom. What's up with that?"

"I'm sorry. I made a mistake," I say, trying to look him in the eye so he'll think I'm telling him the truth.

"Well, yes, you did make a mistake," he says. "But are you trying to tell me that you didn't realize it was the girls' restroom?"

"That's right," I say, nodding. "I forgot to read the sign on the door."

"And what about all your classmates who were gathered in the hall?" he asks. "High-fiving you and so on. Was that a mistake, too?"

WHOA! Are there spy cameras in the halls, now?

"Let me tell you what *I* think happened," the principal says, not waiting for me to answer his question. "I think it was a dare, Mr. Jakes. I think one of the other boys dared you to go in there, and you took him up on it."

"But nobody in the girls' restroom got embarrassed," I tell him quickly. "We made sure of that."

"We?" he asks, pouncing on the word.

Oops. "I meant '*me*,'" I tell him, because I don't want to get Annie Pat and Emma in trouble, too. Or Jared and Stanley, either. Because what good would that do?

Also, I'd *never* get my dad's smoky quartz crystal back if I told on Jared.

The principal stops petting his beard. He clears his throat. "Ms. Sanchez told me all about the situation with your father's crystals, EllRay," he says.

Whoa. What a squealer she is!

"But why?" I say, and it comes out like a squawk.

"That's between my dad and me, and I'm trying to make it right."

"Glad to hear it," the principal says. "And I applaud you for those efforts, but not when they affect your behavior at Oak Glen."

"I know. I'm sorry," I tell him again.

But really, I'm starting to feel kind of mad.

"Why did you give your father's crystals away?" the principal says.

"Ms. Sanchez already asked me that," I tell him. "I just got a little excited, that's all. I'm only *eight*," I remind him, trying for once to look even smaller than I already am, which is pretty small.

"But what were you hoping to get in return?" the principal asks.

"Respect!" I say, and thunder booms outside.

"You have to earn respect," the principal says. "You can't buy it by carrying out dares or giving away crystals, EllRay."

"But how are you supposed to earn respect when you don't have anything to earn it *with*?" I ask him, my words tumbling out like those little candies in the machine at the supermarket—the machine that always gives you the wrong color candy, as if by magic. "I'm too short to be chosen first in sports," I say, pointing out the obvious. "And I'm not all that great at anything yet except having fun, to tell the truth. So I was trying to use my dad's stuff to get respect, the way everyone else in my class does lately. The boys, anyway. But the whole thing backfired."

"Ah," the principal says.

"I wanted the kids to see how great my dad is," I say. "Even though he'll never buy a humongous TV like Corey's dad or an ATV with flames on it like Jared's dad."

"Some kids do a lot of bragging about their folks in primary school, even these days," the principal agrees. "Just the way some kids do a lot of complaining about them in middle school and high school. But you have to learn to stand alone, Mr. Jakes—and be judged on your own merits."

I don't really know what he's trying to say, so I keep my mouth shut. That is usually the best thing to do at times like these.

Just another hint!

The principal laughs. "You're a good kid, EllRay.

And you—*you*—have a **LOT** to be proud of now."

"Like what?" I mumble, staring down at my sneakers.

"Like, you're a good friend," he says. "For instance, look how loyal you're being to the other kids involved in that restroom caper. And you try to make things right when you mess up. That takes guts."

"I mess up a lot," I admit reluctantly. "So I guess I have lots of guts inside me."

"Everyone makes mistakes," the principal says. "But not everyone takes responsibility for their mistakes the way you do. You're a stand-up guy. I admire you, Mr. Jakes. I think your father is a very lucky man."

I peek at him to see if he is joking. He looks pretty serious, but it's hard to tell with that beard covering so much of his face. "You do?" I finally ask.

He nods. "I do," he tells me. "But I want you to promise me that you'll stay out of the girls' restroom—for at least another week."

Now, he *is* joking. "For the rest of my life," I promise.

"Well, okay then," he says.

"Are you gonna tell my parents?" I ask, looking out the window at the rain.

"Oh," he says, "I think we can keep this between us, don't you?"

And I nod yes, of course, because I really, really think we can.

Really.

17

VALENTINE'S DAY

My mom is amazed when I say we have to leave early for school today because I need her to drive me to the supermarket. "Why?" she asks.

"I gotta buy something," I mumble. "With my saved-up allowance and Christmas money."

Alfie is listening in, naturally.

"Lancelot Raymond Jakes," my mom says, frowning. "Don't you dare tell me I was supposed to make cupcakes for that party today."

"We get to have cupcakes too, at my day care, 'cause it's Valentine's Day," Alfie says, almost drooling at the breakfast table. "Pink, with chocolate sprinkles, I hope."

"It's not cupcakes," I tell Mom. "It's flowers. I have to buy this special kind of flowers for someone."

"Oh, *EllRay*," my mom says, her brown eyes

shining with romance and other embarrassing things. "Of course I can take you to the store. Who are the flowers for, honey? Or is it a great big secret?"

"Are they for me?" Alfie asks, frowning. "Because I like candy best, not toopid flowers."

"They're for someone at school, okay?" I say, thinking that Cynthia would be really happy to see me suffering so much just because of her—and because of that tourmaline, which she handed over first thing yesterday morning.

I'll give her that much credit.

"I know. They're for Ms. Sanchez," my mom says like she has solved a riddle. She sounds thrilled. "Well, I think that's just about the sweetest thing I ever heard."

"They're not for Ms. Sanchez," I say, trying not to yell.

"Then they're for **SOME GIRL,**" Alfie exclaims. "Ooo," she says, and she starts kissing the back of her hand again and again.

"EllRay," Mom says, astonished. "Really?"

"Don't get all excited," I tell her gloomily. "It's not what you think."

But I can't tell her I'm bringing flowers to school because I'm basically being blackmailed, can I? She'd get even *more* excited, then. And not in a good way.

My dad walks into the kitchen like he's going someplace important, and he kisses my mom and pours himself a cup of coffee. "Today's the day," he says.

As if any of us needed reminding.

"It certainly is, Warren," my mom says, and she instantly changes his mood by putting his coffee cup on the counter, then whirling him around the kitchen in a pretend dance.

"Me too!" Alfie cries, trying to jam herself between them.

"I'm gonna just go brush my teeth," I tell everyone, but I don't think they hear me.

× × ×

"Good morning, ladies and gentlemen," Ms. Sanchez says above the excited, special-day buzz everyone is making. "And happy Valentine's Day!"

The girls are all dressed up, of course, but the boys just look normal.

All except me, because I'm the kid who's holding a drippy bunch of blue flowers in his lap. And now there's glitter all over my pants. I'll probably sparkle all day long.

Thanks a lot, Cynthia.

"As you know," Ms. Sanchez says, "we won't be opening our valentines until the end of class, when we'll also be having a little party, thanks to our wonderful parent volunteers. But it looks as though EllRay has a special valentine that just can't wait. EllRay?" she says, sounding both encouraging and ready to thank me.

She thinks the flowers are for her.

And so does everyone else. *Almost* everyone.

Cynthia and Heather are grinning like crazy, of course.

Well, I might as well get this over with. I walk to the front of the class. "These are for—for Cynthia Harbison," I say, forcing myself to say her name, and I **SQUINCH** my eyes shut like a bolt of lightning is about to strike me down right here in front of Ms. Sanchez and her third grade class. "Happy Valentine's Day, Cynthia," I manage to add, in case Cynthia thinks that's part of the deal.

Ms. Sanchez—and most of the other kids—look totally stunned.

"For *me*?" Cynthia squeals, gasping to show how surprised she is, and she races to the front of the class like she's got little jet engines in her shoes.

What a faker!

"Take 'em," I mutter, and she does.

"Oh, thanks," she exclaims, and head down, I hurry back to my seat before she even *thinks* of hugging or kissing me, in case that was part of her terrible plan. "I don't know what to say," Cynthia continues, looking as though she's about to start saying a *lot*. It's as if she's just won a huge award or something.

"You don't need to say a thing," Ms. Sanchez tells her briskly. "Please take your seat, and we'll put those flowers in some water right after I finish taking attendance."

I think Ms. Sanchez knows exactly what happened.

I just hope the other kids do, too. Especially the boys.

“Okay,” Cynthia says, looking sorry that she can’t drag out her minute of glory a little longer. “Ohh,” she says, sniffing the flowers noisily as she goes back to her seat.

I hope she gets glitter up her nose!

“Dude,” Kevin whispers to me, looking confused and disappointed. “Dude.”

“I’ll tell you later,” I whisper back.

* 18 *

PROUD

"That was some fancy bunch of flowers you gave Cynthia this morning," Ms. Sanchez says that afternoon at the Valentine's Day party, after taking a dainty nibble of her pink-frosted cupcake.

We also have pink lemonade to drink. This is a very girly celebration, in my opinion, but the food's good if you close your eyes and forget about the color.

"I assume it was a trade?" Ms. Sanchez asks. "For her crystal?"

I take a huge bite of my cupcake, because I can't figure out whether or not this is a trick question. Will I get in trouble again if I answer it? Or if I *don't* answer it? Or will I get Cynthia in trouble?

Sometimes it's tough being me!

"I dunno," I finally say, hoping I don't have a

dab of frosting on my nose—the way Cynthia does. **SCORE**.

She just went prancing by holding her flowers.

"And can I assume a few lessons have been learned?" Ms. Sanchez asks, but she sounds more jokey than strict.

So I get up enough nerve to say, "Excuse me, but do you mean *are you physically able* to assume that?" Just to tease her.

Maybe it's the sugar, like my mom's always saying.

"Point taken, Mr. Jakes," Ms. Sanchez says, laughing. "*May* I assume a few lessons have been learned?"

"You may," I say, eyeing the few leftover cupcakes on the long table.

"You're something else, do you know that?" she tells me, still smiling.

And however she means what she just said, I decide to take it as a compliment. "Thanks," I say, smiling back at her. "You too. Happy Valentine's Day, Ms. Sanchez."

× × ×

It is now Friday night, and my mom and my dad—who counted and inspected every crystal yesterday, and then shook my hand and actually hugged me tight—are busy getting ready to go out for dinner. Mom made a special dinner for Alfie and me. She even got two DVDs for us to chose from, with Monique, our sitter, acting as referee.

Monique's okay. She knows how to crack her knuckles and dance.

I just put Alfie's "required valentine" on her dinner plate, and I'm pretty sure she'll like it.

1. Her valentine is at least four times as big as the one I made for Mom.
2. It shows two fuzzy kittens sitting in a basket, and Alfie loves kittens, big surprise.
3. And there is paper lace all around the edges.
4. Also, I used silver duct tape to stick two candy bars onto it!

Alfie comes sneaking into the kitchen with her hands behind her back. "Happy Valentine's Day, EllWay," she says, mispronouncing my name as usual. And then she hands me something.

It's a crystal!

A purple amethyst.

"But *shhh.* Don't tell Daddy," she whispers. "I went into his office and took it. But he's got tons, so that's all wight."

"Alfie," I say, "it's *not* all wight. I mean, all *right.* We gotta put this back fast!"

If Dad gets mad again, he might cancel our secret shopping trip tomorrow. The one for the spray paint, where I get to choose the colors.

Yellow, orange, and purple, by the way.

"I don't want to," she says, her face puckering up the way it does when she's about to cry. "It's your *valentine.*"

"This crystal is Dad's private property," I tell my little sister, trying to keep my voice quiet. "But it's the thought that counts," I say quickly, and she cheers up pretty fast. "Thanks, Alfie. Now, let's go."

And we tiptoe down the hall toward Dad's office and put the crystal back on his display shelf, then we creep back toward the kitchen like bad guys on a TV crime show.

"Where's *my* valentine?" Alfie asks when we get back to the kitchen. And then she spots it. "Yay-y-y!" she shouts, clasping the big lumpy card to her chest. "And it's got candy bars on it! My favorite kinds, too!"

"I hope you like it," I tell her, trying to sound modest.

Actually, I hope she'll *share*, but I'm not exactly holding my breath.

Mom and Dad bustle into the room just as there's a knock on the door. "Well, isn't that nice of your big brother," Dad says to Alfie about the big valentine, while Mom goes to greet the sitter. "Good job, son. I'm proud of you. For a whole lot of reasons," he adds, giving me a special look.

"You are?" I ask, suddenly feeling kind of shy. Shy, around my own dad!

"I am," he says, nodding his head.

"And me too, Daddy?" Alfie says, horning in as usual.

"You too, baby girl," he says, nuzzling her neck.

But he shoots me another special look, and I feel really good.

"Now, you children behave," my mom tells Alfie and me as they get ready to go out the door for their probably-smoochy dinner. "And you mind Monique, hear?"

"Okay, Mommy," Alfie says, giving Mom a final hug.

"Okay," I say too, and I sound a lot more confident than I usually do when I make this babysitter promise.

But I'm not gonna go getting in trouble again. Not so close to last time.

NO WAY!